Boyfriend
for hire

New York Times & *USA Today* Bestselling Author
KENDALL RYAN

Boyfriend for Hire
Copyright © 2019 Kendall Ryan

Content Editing by
Elaine York

Copy Editing by
Pam Berehulke

Cover Design and Formatting by
Uplifting Designs

About the Book

I'm the guy you call when you need to impress your overbearing family, your boss, or your ex. Yeah, I'm a male escort, but not just any escort, I'm *the* escort. The one with a mile-long waiting list and a pristine reputation that's very well-deserved.

I'm the guy who'll make you feel beautiful, desired, and worshipped . . . all for a steep price. I'm hired to make you shine, and I always deliver.

I'll be whatever you want me to be for one night—except my true self. This is just a job, a role I play to earn a paycheck.

But I'm not the guy who falls for a client. Not once in six years.

And then I meet Elle. Her friend has hired me to escort her to a wedding, but Elle doesn't know we're just pretending.

There's a fire between us I never expected. A connection I haven't felt in so long. One kiss, and I'm losing all control.

But what will happen when she finds out who I really am?

Chapter One

Nic

I pull up outside the mini-mansion and check my reflection in the mirror. Dressed in a tailored black suit with a crisp white shirt, I know I look good . . . actually, better than good. It's not being cocky if it's true, and I was blessed with good genetics. That's just a fact of life.

After closing the visor, I slip my sunglasses inside my jacket pocket and climb from my shiny black Tesla, ready to get on with my workday.

I let myself inside and head through the marble foyer of Case's home. He runs the Allure agency out of his home office, but this place is so large, I swear he doesn't even notice that at any given time there are at least two or three guys hanging out here, eating his food, drinking his beer, or using his home gym. It's basically become a male-escort headquarters in an unsuspecting neighborhood in an upscale suburb of Chicago.

Inside, I find Ryder, Case's right hand and best friend . . . and a fellow escort.

"Hey, dude," I say. It's just after five, and Ryder's sitting on the couch with a beer in his hand. Doesn't he have to work later too? It's probably not a good sign, but who am I to judge?

"What's up, man?" Ryder says, his gaze still on the football game playing on TV.

"Just stopping by to see Case. Is he in his office?" Even if I haven't seen him yet, I know Case is home. His Mercedes is parked outside.

Ryder grunts something that I think means *yes*, and I head down the hall.

Ryder is playful, fun-loving, and cocky as fuck. Women love him with his bright blue eyes and lightly tanned skin. He's like a walking fantasy with his square jawline and preppy clothes. And the motherfucker's calendar proves it. He's even busier than Case, which is saying something.

Even if Case and Ryder seem happy enough, I know I don't want to end up like them. I don't plan to be a lifer. I'll make money escorting, and then hopefully move on to something else.

Part of me can't believe I've lasted six years doing this. When I met Case and he offered me a job, I scoffed at the idea and blew him off. Then he told me how much I could make—five grand a night—and explained that I wouldn't necessarily have to sleep with anyone for money.

So I said *fuck it* and decided to give it a shot.

I've slept with women I haven't necessarily wanted to sleep with for free, so this is a no-brainer. I figured I'd do it once or twice, take my money, and be done with it.

But the truth is, I couldn't find a job that would even come close to matching this kind of income, and it's spoiled me a bit. Getting to wine and dine beautiful women for a living? It's not exactly a hardship, and even if it were, I'd gladly take one for the team.

Case opened Allure a couple of years before he hired me, and he hasn't slowed down or taken a day off in all that time. The guy's a machine. Tall and commanding, he's able to blend into any social situation with ease. It's a gift, really. Most of the time he's dressed in a suit, but today I find him in a pair of gym shorts and a T-shirt sitting in front of his laptop.

He's as comfortable wining and dining a cougar in a five-star restaurant as he is hanging with us on his couch in sweatpants, scarfing down day-old pizza. Actually, I've looked up to him for a long time. He runs his business with zero drama, pays his taxes, and is able to employ a half dozen of his best friends. It's a pretty sweet deal.

"Hey, what's up?" he asks when he spots me lingering in the doorway to his office.

"Just came to check my schedule for the week."

His gaze lifts from the laptop screen and he smirks. "Yeah, about that. Sit, would you?"

As I sink into the leather chair in front of his desk, an uneasy feeling settles in the pit of my stomach.

"So, I know you're booked with Rebecca from six to nine tonight."

I nod. I met Rebecca three months ago, and now she's a regular. She's an easy client to entertain. As a recently divorced attorney, she has little time for dating, and so twice a month, I fill that void. We go to dinner, and then back to her place where we have vanilla sex. All in all, it's not a hard evening for me. And I leave several grand richer.

"Well, Donovan called in sick tonight. So, after Rebecca, you're meeting Amy at nine thirty. A hotel downtown. I'll text you the address."

I run a hand through my hair and let out a sigh. Entertaining two women in one evening isn't the ideal scenario. "Isn't there someone else?"

Case shakes his head. "Ryder and I are both booked too. Think you can handle a doubleheader?"

I know what he's really asking. Will I be able to get it up and deliver twice within as many hours? "That won't be a problem. But what do you know about Amy?"

Case's firm mouth softens. "You'll like her. Thirty-something, fit, and attractive. She's a single mom who occasionally books with Donovan or Ryder to blow off some steam."

I nod. It's not like I have much of a choice. "Fine."

"Thanks, man." Case looks down at his desk, seeming preoccupied.

"Is that all?" Why do I get the feeling there's something else?

He smirks again. "I know I told you that you'd have tomorrow off, but . . ."

I bite the inside of my cheek. I've been looking forward to sleeping in late tomorrow, hitting the gym, and then spending the afternoon at my apartment's rooftop pool to relax. I've been working too much lately as it is.

"But what?" I ask.

Case leans forward on his elbows. "There's a woman I need you to meet. It's just coffee. Fifteen minutes, tops."

"What's the situation. Why coffee?"

"Guess she wants to meet you before she commits. It happens sometimes," he says with a shrug, then closes his laptop and rises to his feet. "It'll be your job to make her feel comfortable, win her over."

I let out a sigh and stand. "Fine."

Case hands me a sheet of paper that outlines my appointments for the rest of the week. Weekends are busiest, but I still have one or two clients I entertain midweek. I fold the paper and place it inside my jacket pocket, along with my sunglasses.

Since it's almost time to get my evening started, I head out, saying good-bye to Case and then Ryder on my way out.

I really do love my job.

>>——♡——→

Two hours later, I grab the small black duffel bag I keep in my car for work and start up the walk after Rebecca. It contains all the basics—condoms, lube, a variety of vibrators, a silk blindfold, baby wipes, my toothbrush, and a small stash of Viagra.

I've needed help a couple of times to get hard for a client, but thankfully it doesn't happen often. I love sex, and usually the women who book me are attractive socialite types who are bored of their husband and can afford to spend his money on a younger model.

At first, this bothered me—a lot, actually—but then I realized their husbands were doing the same thing—out seeing women half their age, sleeping with their secretaries on the side, basically nailing anything they could catch and release. Once I realized this was the way the game is played in their world, I got along just fine. That isn't to say that sometimes I don't like the feeling of being a pawn in their game. Even if I do support a woman taking charge of her own pleasure, there's still the stigma.

I'd like to think I provide a valuable service. A forty-five-year-old client once told me that she'd never had an orgasm with her husband in twenty-two years of marriage. That's some sad shit right there. I guess this job is just me making up for inadequate men who can't please their ladies. Needless to say, she came four times that first night with me, and continued booking me on and off for over a year until she worked up the courage to ask her husband for a divorce. When she remarried last year, I was invited to her wedding. I didn't go— that would have been weird—but I did send her a toaster. And it was a nice fucking toaster, if I do say so myself.

Dinner with Rebecca is nice, uneventful, and the conversation pleasant. Rebecca always pays, and we always eat at her favorite restaurant, an American bistro with big juicy steaks. Not that I've ever tried one. While I'm working, I try to eat light, knowing the aerobic activities I'll be engaging in later in the evening.

Rebecca shimmies her hips as she walks, her round ass filling out her black pencil skirt nicely. I smirk as I watch her. *No need to seduce me, sweetheart. I'll be fucking you tonight no matter what.*

When she unlocks the door and lets us inside, I'm familiar enough with her fantasies by now that I barely wait for her to close the door behind us. Pressing her against the wall, I devour her neck with kisses.

I never kiss on the mouth, but I have no problem putting my mouth pretty much anywhere else. Well, not *anywhere*. I don't do oral. It's one of the rules I've set for myself. There's something about it that's just so intimate, I'd prefer to save it for someone who means something to me. But Rebecca's interests are pretty tame. She just wants to feel desired. Wants to feel that a man is so enamored with her that he can barely wait until they're inside the bedroom to have her. It's a fantasy I'm happy to act out for her.

I cup her round ass in my palms and give it a squeeze as my teeth nip at her exposed collarbone. It's all very practiced, even if it doesn't seem like it to her.

Her palms explore the contours of my chest beneath my suit jacket, and she makes a pleased sound low in her throat. "Yes, Nic."

My cock hardens as she whimpers and rubs her body against mine.

"Tell me what you want," I whisper against her neck.

Rebecca shivers. "You. My room. Now."

Her bedroom is always immaculately clean, and it smells faintly of lilacs. I waste no time in stripping her down to the black lacy lingerie she always wears for me, and then I'm in my boxer briefs and Rebecca is on her knees in front of me. Thankfully, I'm fully hard now.

While she's never asked me to return the favor, Rebecca usually likes our foreplay to include some time spent with my cock in her mouth. I'm not one to complain about this scenario.

"You're so sexy with my cock in your mouth," I murmur, stroking her hair as I close my eyes.

Thirty minutes later, Rebecca's come twice, and I'm pumping away, sweat dampening my lower back. I glance quickly at her bedside clock to check the time, deciding enough time has passed to allow myself to come. So I finally let go, filling the condom with a sharp exhale.

After a quick visit to the restroom, where I freshen up and dress, I find Rebecca wrapped in her silk sheets, her hair mussed from sex and a satisfied smile on her lips.

"You sure you don't want to stay? I have gelato in my freezer." She grins like we're lovers who have just finished a real date . . . not an impersonal transaction where money exchanges hands.

I'm not sure whether to feel flattered or annoyed. I decide on flattered.

Leaning down to give her ass cheek a squeeze, I shake my head. "Wish I could, darling. I've got plans later."

She nods, her eyes bright and happy. A couple of orgasms will do that to a woman. "Okay. Good night then, Nic."

"Good night."

I release a sigh as I head back down the walk, duffel in hand, toward my car.

One down; one left to go tonight.

And tomorrow, on what's supposed to be my day off, Case has me working. Some coffee date. *At least it won't be sex* crosses my mind as I start the engine to head to appointment number two.

Jesus, what man in his right mind thinks "at least it won't be sex" without needing to visit a mental health professional for a complete checkup? I'm thinking I really need a day off.

Chapter Two

Nic

L ast night's activities wore me out more than usual, and I'm running a couple of minutes behind, which isn't like me. I generally like to arrive to a date early, to give myself time to scope everything out and best plan how to approach things.

But this isn't technically a *date*, I remind myself. Just some woman who wants to prescreen me before agreeing to fake-date me.

I park my car and glance at the coffee shop, wondering if she's already inside. I try to recall what Case told me about my date today, and realize he didn't tell me much at all. Just the name Christine, which was printed on the sheet he gave me, along with the time and location of the appointment.

Here goes nothing.

I stroll into the coffee shop and find it mostly deserted, given that it's early afternoon and the morning caffeine rush is over. It makes spotting Christine very easy. There are a few tables containing couples, and one with a group of elderly women, but only one with a single woman seated by herself.

She looks up when she hears the chimes over the door, and when our eyes lock, her mouth softens in a smile. As I approach the table where she's seated, I have to say I'm pleasantly surprised. She's close to my own age of twenty-eight, and she looks nice. Normal. That's always a positive in my line of work.

"Christine?" I ask, pulling out the chair across from her. She's attractive with dark hair, brown eyes, and straight white teeth.

She gives me a shy smile and a quick nod. "And you're Nic?"

"It's nice to meet you. May I sit?"

She gestures to the chair across from her. "Of course. Please do. Thank you for meeting me. I'm not sure if this is how it normally goes, or . . ."

I offer her a polite smile. "This can go however you want it to. My goal is to make sure you're comfortable. And there's not just one way to approach it."

This seems to relax her, and she takes a deep breath.

I can't help but notice the rather large engagement ring sparkling on her ring finger. Engagement, not wedding ring. Hmm . . .

"Would you like something to drink," she asks. "Coffee, or . . ."

I shake my head. "I'm good. If I drink coffee at this time of day, I won't be able to sleep tonight." I don't tell her that I usually sleep like shit anyway, so it probably wouldn't matter much.

"Right." She nods, her face going serious. "I guess let's just get on with this."

Leaning closer, I offer her another smile. "Why don't you tell me what it is I can help you with. My clients come to me for a variety of reasons, and you have nothing to be ashamed of. I'm more than happy to help in any way I can. It's my job. But if you don't like what you hear from me and decide this isn't for you, then no harm, no foul. Okay?"

She smiles again, brighter this time. "Oh, you'll be perfect. I have no doubt about that." Her gaze wanders from mine to my left dimple, and then down to my broad shoulders and the muscular biceps visible below the short sleeves of my T-shirt.

I still have no fucking idea what we're talking about when she grabs her phone and pulls up a picture of a girl and holds it up for me to see. The girl is fucking stunning with long red hair, a full pouty mouth, and curves for days.

"This is my friend Elle. Well, my soon-to-be sister-in-law, actually." Christine's gaze falls to her engagement ring, and her smile brightens. "I love her like a sister, and there's nothing I wouldn't do for her."

"I'm sorry, what? Is the date for you or for her?"

"Oh, it's for her. My wedding is next weekend, and . . ." Christine puts her phone away and her smile falters. "Her dickhead ex recently broke up with her, leaving her without a date. But worse than that, he's still planning on coming to the wedding, and bringing the new girlfriend he started dating about three seconds after he and Elle broke up."

"He sounds like a twat."

Christine giggles. "Oh, he is. But he and my fiancé grew up together, and it's not like we can uninvite him now without making it a big thing."

"So, you want me to escort Elle to the wedding?"

She nods. "Yes. Only, I don't want her to know you're a . . . that you . . . I told her I have a friend from college I can set her up with."

"I see." So she won't know I'm an escort. A little unusual, but I can work with that.

"And it's just to accompany her. I'm not paying extra for the . . . you know." She leans closer and whispers, "Sex."

I chuckle and place one hand on the table, not bothering to explain to her that I don't always have sex with clients. It does happen on occasion, but I'm not a prostitute, for fuck's sake. Plenty of times it's just a night out. "No worries. I understand. So, the wedding is next Saturday?"

Christine nods. "Yes, but there's also a cocktail reception for out-of-town guests on Friday that Elle will be expected to attend. I was hoping to have you for Friday and Saturday nights."

"That will cost extra, but it can be arranged."

Christine nods. "I'm aware of your fees. That's not an issue. But you'll need a suit for Friday and a tux for Saturday . . ."

I hold up one hand, stopping her. "It's not a problem. I'll be dressed appropriately."

"Thank you so much for agreeing to do this." Christine's posture relaxes for the first time since I sat down.

"I'm happy to do it. I love weddings." Cake. Dancing. Everyone in a happy mood. It'll be the easiest money I've ever made.

Christine hands me a sleek white wedding invitation embossed with gold script and rises to her feet. "Oh, and since I told Elle that you're a friend of mine from college, I went, um, I mean *we* went to the University of Indiana."

I lift one eyebrow. I've never been to Indiana and I certainly never went to college, something I still regret, but I nod. "Sounds good. Anything else?"

She shakes her head. "I kept it simple. We fell out of touch but recently connected again on social media when we saw we both lived here now."

I stand and face Christine, glancing briefly at

the invitation. "I'll see you Friday at six."

She nods. "One last thing. Do you mind if I take a picture of you on my phone to show Elle? You know, to make it seem more normal and get her to agree to the date."

"Sure." I smile as Christine poses beside me and snaps a quick selfie of us together.

"Thanks for this, Nic."

"My pleasure."

As I stroll out of the coffee shop, I realize that I'm actually looking forward to the wedding next weekend. Sweet young Elle won't know what hit her.

Chapter Three

Elle

Yoga. I really need to take up yoga. It's probably the only thing that will keep me from sucker punching my ex in the dick today. This is the thought that pervades my brain as I inspect my lipstick in the gilded bathroom mirror of the country club.

Sighing, I check my reflection one last time and smooth my hair. I know black is supposed to be slimming, so why does it feel like I've stuffed myself inside a sausage casing? Why do I feel like a busted can of biscuits in this getup?

Ugh. Breathe, Elle.

"God blessed you with these amazing curves. Don't hide them." Christine turns to face me, the corners of her mouth pulled down. It's like she can read my mind.

I roll my eyes. "I couldn't hide them even if I wanted to. My Spanx are earning every dime I spent on them."

She squeezes my hand. "Stop stressing. You'll like Nic. And he'll be speechless with you on his arm, I promise."

I've never been set up on a blind date before, and I'm not sure how it's going to go. I've been a nervous wreck all day, and the fact that my asshole ex is going to be at this cocktail reception with his new stick-figure girlfriend isn't helping calm my nerves.

It's the day before my friend Christine's wedding, and she happens to be marrying my brother. So as much as I'd like to lock myself in my room all weekend with a pint of peanut butter ice cream and a bottle of vodka, I know I have to be here for them. Adulting really, really sucks sometimes.

Christine gives my shoulder an encouraging pat.

I keep telling myself that if I can get through this cocktail party tonight and the wedding and reception tomorrow, I can move on and pretend this whole weekend never happened.

After she finishes touching up her lipstick, Christine and I leave the bathroom and wander into the main ballroom. I grab a glass of champagne from one of the servers passing around drinks while she says good-bye and heads over to rejoin my brother. Taking a long sip, I enjoy the sensation of the bubbles on my tongue. I'm a lightweight and never have more than two drinks, but this weekend might be the exception.

I round the corner in search of a familiar friendly face, but instead I spot Jeremy, my ex. I quickly jump back and flatten myself against the wall, but not before I catch a glimpse of his new girlfriend hanging on his arm.

I've seen her on social media—and by seen, I mean I've stalked her—but I'm not pleased to see she's even more attractive in person. She's tall and unbelievably skinny, wearing a formfitting red dress. I'm not overweight, but I am curvy, and I could never pull off a skintight dress like his new girlfriend is wearing, even if I starved myself for a week.

Jeremy and I have known each other for a long time, but I was always the nerdy little sister of his best friend. After college, he finally took notice, and we dated for two years. I'd had a crush on him for so long that I realize now that I overlooked a lot of the flaws in our relationship. I thought he was the one, but then he broke up with me out of the blue. One minute he was telling me he loved me, and the next he was saying he needed time alone to "find himself." Which couldn't have been true, because three seconds later he was dating someone else. *Dick.*

I take a large sip of champagne just as he bends down and gives her a kiss on the cheek. It takes every ounce of willpower I have to force myself to swallow. I'm definitely going to need more than two drinks to deal with this.

I glance at my watch. My date should be walking in the door any minute. When Christine told me she had an old friend from college she wanted to set me up with, I was skeptical, to say the least. But the thought of attending this wedding alone with Jeremy here was too much, so I agreed. The last thing I need is to look like some pathetic loser in front of the happy couple—and I'm not referring to my brother and his fiancée.

As I take another glance at the door, someone walks in, and I let out a small gasp. I know immediately that it's the guy from the photo Christine sent me, but that picture didn't do him justice.

He scans the room, running a hand through his messy brown hair, and my heart begins to beat in overdrive. A bit of facial hair accentuates his perfect jawline and full lips. He's wearing a classic black suit that accentuates his broad chest and narrow hips.

I've never seen someone as attractive as him outside of fashion magazines, and he looks like he could easily have come from a red-carpet event. I realize I've been staring with my mouth open and force myself to close it, hoping no one saw my ogling.

The room is loud, but all of it fades away when he looks in my direction. She must have shown him a picture of me too, because he smiles when he sees me and walks toward me. My heart pounds harder with each step closer he takes.

"Elle?"

When he looks into my eyes, my stomach starts flipping like an Olympic gymnast. His chocolate-brown eyes are so mesmerizing, I have to force myself to look away from them. But as my gaze wanders to his mouth again, I realize that isn't going to help my pounding heart.

"Nic, right?" I ask after a brief pause.

He nods, smiling to reveal perfectly straight white teeth. His eyes light up with something like mischief or amusement. But either way, he has my full attention.

Nic holds out a hand, and when I place my palm in his, a tingle runs up my arm.

"Thanks for coming," I say, smiling awkwardly.

"My pleasure." His voice is deep and sexy, perfect for dirty talk during sex.

Elle, get a hold of yourself.

"Your picture didn't do you justice. You look amazing." He sounds sincere, and I can't help but melt a little.

"You look great too." I smile, looking him up and down again. If the way his suit fits is any indication of his physique, he's got the body of a Greek god. "So, you know Christine from Indiana?" I ask, tearing my gaze away from his broad shoulders.

"Yeah, we had a few classes together." He smiles.

Grinning back, I say, "From what I hear, she didn't do much studying in college." Christine has a lot of wild stories from her college years. I was too focused on studying and preparing for law school to do much partying myself, but I always enjoyed hearing about all the crazy things she and her friends did.

"Yeah, we got into some trouble." He laughs, running his hand through his hair again.

How is he so damn sexy? Just watching him makes me feel like I've committed a sin.

Nic's smile fades, and his expression turns serious. "I never expected that when I reached out to her, she'd end up inviting me to her wedding. Or that she'd set me up with such a beautiful date."

I gulp. So he's sexy, nice, and polite? I'm crushing hard on this guy.

"Speaking of getting into trouble, would you like a drink?" I gesture toward the bar.

His lips twitch. "Absolutely."

As we walk, I notice how tall he is, easily a couple of inches over six feet. His height makes me feel small and dainty, a feeling I could really get used to.

Nic orders himself a whiskey neat from the bartender, and pauses to ask what I'd like. I lift my half-empty glass of champagne to request another.

Just as I'm about to ask Nic more about his college years, Jeremy walks toward us.

"Fuck," I whisper, turning toward Nic.

"Is something wrong?" he asks as the bartender sets down our drinks.

"My ex is walking this way right now," I say, wishing I could disappear. I glance at Nic. "We had a rough breakup, in case Christine didn't mention anything to you."

Nic nods, furrowing his brow. I hope that seeing me react like this to my ex isn't scaring him off. It's not exactly a turn-on to have your date freak out over another guy.

"Sorry—" I say, but Nic cuts me off.

"Just follow my lead," he says and starts laughing loudly.

Startled, I just stare for a second.

"Laugh," he whispers to me.

Finally, I get the hint and start to laugh along with him just as Jeremy walks up to the bar. I can see him out of the corner of my eye look over at us.

Nic sets his drink down and lifts his hand to smooth a stray strand of hair away from my face.

When he touches me, it's like the whole world stops. As Nic tucks my hair behind my ear, I forget all about Jeremy and take a deep, shaky breath, feeling like I've been sucker punched in the stomach.

As Nic stares deeply into my eyes, my knees start to feel shaky. With him standing so close, I catch a hint of his scent, something earthy and masculine, totally intoxicating. His full lips curve into a smile, and I'm totally lost in the moment when Nic breaks eye contact to glance at where Jeremy was standing. He's gone, and Nic turns back to me, grinning. I didn't even noticed he left.

"I think we pulled that off," Nic says with a grin.

I smile back weakly. He probably has no idea how much he's affecting me right now, or that I couldn't care less what Jeremy thought of that moment, only that I want it to happen again.

"Thanks," I say, shocked at how sweet Nic is. Usually, guys as hot as he is don't try this hard because they know they can get any girl they want. Briefly, I wonder if he has some horrible flaw that's going to rear its ugly head later. It would be just my luck. I overlooked so many things about Jeremy, and I won't make that same mistake again.

"Cheers to meeting new people—and avoiding ones we know." Nic holds up his whiskey, and we clink glasses.

"Sorry this is kind of awkward with my ex here," I say, afraid Nic's going to decide this is too much drama. After what I just felt, I don't think I could stand it if he bailed on the weekend. "Christine probably didn't warn you about that part."

"She didn't mention it, but it's not a problem. I know how shitty breakups can be," he says, leaning back against the bar. "Just consider me your personal bodyguard. Who is also your drinking buddy for the weekend."

"A man of many talents." Relieved, I grin. "Lucky me."

"You have no idea." He smirks, taking a sip of his whiskey.

I can think of a couple other talents you might have.

Looking him up and down again, I take a breath, trying to keep my thoughts focused on the conversation and not on what he could do for me in the bedroom.

"I also dance," he says, saving me from my

wayward thoughts.

"You might be on your own for that one." I smile politely, finishing my champagne. "I'm a horrible dancer."

"Oh, I didn't say I was good. And if I'm going to make a fool of myself on the dance floor, you're definitely coming with me."

We laugh, and as he runs a hand through his dark hair again, I notice for the first time how big his hands are. I bite my lip, trying not to let my mind wander to all the places I want him to put those hands.

His laugh is deep and sexy, almost like a growl. Everything about him is sinful, and I feel like I'm riding on a high. Maybe the champagne is going to my head, but I don't think so. Something about Nic is different from any other guy I've ever met. He's so confident and at ease, both with himself and with me, and it's a huge turn-on.

A server comes around and tells us it's time to head in for dinner. After we're seated at our table, the speeches begin, and everyone toasts with champagne to the bride and groom. I lock eyes with Christine and she gives me a huge smile, obviously pleased to see Nic and me together.

As the server sets down my meal, I suddenly feel ravenous. I was so nervous about seeing Jeremy tonight, and with my anxiety over this blind date, I couldn't eat anything all day, and believe me, I never skip meals. I take a big bite of chicken and let out a groan, but when I realize Nic is watching me, I'm so embarrassed, I stop.

"I didn't eat much today," I say, feeling the need to apologize. Jeremy always used to comment on what I ate, and it made me self-conscious about eating in front of guys.

"You should never apologize for that," Nic says earnestly, and I'm totally spellbound by how understanding and sweet he is. Then he grins. "Besides, I like a woman who knows what she wants."

"I'm sure you do," I say, smirking at him.

Nic tilts his head as he studies me, then chuckles. "You're something else, you know that?"

"But, seriously, I don't normally eat like I've been starved for two days," I say, hoping to get back to a topic with less sexual subtext. "I've just been a little anxious today. I wasn't exactly looking forward to this night. No offense," I add quickly.

"None taken," he says. "So, what exactly did this guy do to fuck up your relationship?"

I look down at the table as memories of our breakup come rushing back.

"He broke up with me, actually," I say, then take a large gulp of champagne.

If I'm going to tell the sexiest man I've ever met about how I was dumped and replaced by another woman, I need a little liquid courage. Well, if I'm honest, I need a lot of liquid courage to admit that I was dumped.

"It was pretty much out of nowhere. And then a few days later, I see that he's got a new girlfriend." I gesture across the room to where Jeremy is sitting with her.

I've been trying not to look at them all night, but I can't help but stare for a few seconds as he whispers something in her ear, making her laugh.

"You're way more beautiful than she is, you know," Nic says, catching me off guard.

My face warms, partly from embarrassment that he saw me staring at them, and partly because I've never had a guy as drop-dead gorgeous as him even look at me, never mind tell me I'm beautiful. Especially after watching me shovel my dinner in my mouth like a ravenous buzzard.

"Thanks," I say, smiling. "Even though I think you're a liar."

"Seriously, you have no idea what a catch you are."

When Nic covers my hand with his, my heart thumps hard as his brown eyes look warmly into mine. I'm speechless, and luckily the moment is interrupted by Christine coming over to say hello. I tear my gaze away from Nic to smile at her.

"You look amazing," I say, jumping up to give her a hug.

"Christine, congratulations again," Nic says.

I don't know if that moment affected him as much as it did me, but he seems completely calm, so it must be my imagination.

"Thanks for coming, Nic. It's good to see you again." She smiles at him before looking back at me. I can tell she's dying to hear about how we're getting along.

"I'm going to use the restroom," I say, giving Christine a meaningful look.

"I'll come too," she says quickly.

"Nic, do you think you'll be okay for a few

minutes?" I ask, grabbing my purse.

"Take your time." He gives me a knowing smile, so I'm pretty sure he knows exactly what we're about to go do.

As soon as the door to the restroom closes, Christine turns to me. "So, how's it going with Nic?"

"He's amazing, Chris." I gush over him as I check my makeup in the mirror. "Seriously, you didn't tell me how hot he is. And he's so sweet. Why have you kept him from me for so long?"

She laughs. "You were with Jeremy. And Nic just recently moved here to Chicago."

"Speaking of Jeremy," I say, then fill her in on the run-in with him, and how Nic just told me Jeremy's new girlfriend doesn't hold a candle to me.

"He's right. You are more beautiful than her," Christine says. "I know Jeremy is your brother's good friend, but he's an asshole and you deserve better. You have to know that, because it's the truth."

I smile at her, then give her another hug. She's always had a talent for seeing the best in me, and knows exactly how to cheer me up in a tough situation.

"I'm so glad you're having fun." Christine smiles, pulling me in tighter. "I just want you to have a good time and not worry about Jeremy and his date."

I've been trying not to let her know how much I was dreading the weekend, not wanting to ruin her special day, but of course she saw right through me.

"Trust me, I'm barely even thinking about Jeremy," I tell her, and I mean it.

I've only known Nic for an hour, but it feels like much longer. How is it possible that a guy this sexy, smart, funny, and sweet even exists? And that he isn't already attached to another woman? It seems almost too good to be true.

"I just want you to remember that you're amazing and deserve the best," Christine says, checking her makeup.

"You're gonna make me cry." I slap her playfully on the shoulder. "Now, let's get back out there before they send a search party for us."

As we leave the restroom, my gaze is immediately drawn to Nic. I'm blown away again by how gorgeous he is. How is it that each time I look at him, he gets more attractive?

He looks my way and our eyes meet, sending me into a full swoon. Everything else fades away as I walk toward him, and all the past drama with Jeremy seems like it happened to someone else.

If someone told me a week ago that I'd actually be looking forward to this wedding, I'd have thought they were crazy. But something about Nic sets off butterflies in my stomach like I'm in the seventh grade all over again.

I've always been a goody-two-shoes, always doing exactly what's expected of me. I pay my bills on time. I obey traffic laws, even if there's no one else around. And I always eat my vegetables, even when I don't want to.

But as I return to Nic, I decide that I'm tired of being a goody-goody. I want to do something reckless for once.

And I have a feeling he may be the perfect guy to get into trouble with.

Chapter Four

Nic

"So, basically, you saw this wedding coming from a mile away," I say, draping my arm over the back of Elle's chair.

We've been chatting easily through dinner and have just started dessert. It hasn't been difficult to find things to talk about, especially once I hit the jackpot of something to discuss when I brought up the relationship between her brother and soon-to-be sister-in-law.

A small smile lifts the corner of Elle's mouth and she crosses a leg toward me, leaning into the closeness I've invited between us.

"I guess you could say I'm a psychic or something," she murmurs, her eyes bright and playful.

She's cute. Way damn cuter than I expected.

And sexy. Part of me wonders why Christine even felt the need to hire me. Elle's luck with men can't possibly be that bad, not when she's getting into my head so easily.

Unfortunately, I don't have to wait long to remember why she's currently single.

Out of the corner of my eye, I see a dark figure moving toward us. Before I can respond to Elle's outlandish and adorable-as-hell claim, a cold, condescending voice interrupts us.

"Are you sure you want to be eating that cake, Elle?"

I look up to find her asshole ex looming over us, raising his eyebrows at the half-eaten slice on her plate. The blood drains from Elle's face and she sets her fork down, self-consciously wiping the corner of her mouth with her napkin.

"Well, it is a damn good cake. It's a celebration, isn't it?" I ask, my voice light but my eyes steely.

I don't want to make a scene, but I'll be damned if this asshat thinks he's about to ruin this date. I'm a professional, for fuck's sake. Women pay me to make *sure* they have a good time, and I'll be damned if this fuckwad is going to rain on Elle's parade.

And this isn't just about Elle. What kind of man would I be if I stood by and allowed this to happen? One prick in an ill-fitting suit isn't about to ruin my track record either. He's several inches shorter than me, and his hair is thinning on top. On those merits alone, he's no prize catch.

"Between you and me, pal, she's been trying to lose weight for the better part of three years. And judging by the fit of that dress," he pauses to give Elle a once-over, "it's not going well." He claps a firm hand on my shoulder and turns to stroll away.

Before he can leave, I stand, gripping his arm and holding him in place. "Where the fuck do you get off, man?"

His gaze passes over Elle before returning to me. "Not on that anymore." He smirks as he glances back in Elle's direction, shaking himself free from my grasp.

"I don't know how the fuck you were raised, but this isn't how you treat a woman."

He doesn't respond, and his expression stays neutral as he walks away to join his scrawny new girlfriend across the room.

My fists clench at my sides as I draw on every ounce of restraint I possess not to march over there and show that prick what a piece of shit he is. But I don't want to make a scene at Christine's party. It would only make Elle uncomfortable. Instead, I take a deep breath and force myself to relax.

I straighten my tie and glance at Elle to make sure she's okay. "You all right?"

"I will be." She draws a deep breath, letting it out slowly through her nostrils. I can tell she's on the verge of tears and doing everything she can to hold it in.

"He's wrong, you know."

Her gaze snaps to mine. "About what?"

Placing one hand against the small of her back, I lean in closer and drop my voice lower, just barely above a whisper. "Your curves are sexy as hell."

The pulse in her throat strums steadily, but she presses her lips together and gives her head a small shake. "Don't do that. Don't try to make me feel better by telling me what you think I want to hear."

My thumb slides along her spine, rubbing the bare skin exposed by her scooped neckline. I feel her skin pebble in goose bumps.

"I wouldn't say it if it weren't true. I promise, when I laid eyes on you, I had a hard time keeping my thoughts clean. Trust me, what was running through my mind was anything but gentlemanly. You're sexy as fuck, Elle."

Her breathing stutters and her gaze swings to mine, wide and curious. "Um, thank you? You are too . . . um, sexy, I mean. Not curvy. I don't think men are supposed to be curvy, though. More like muscular and fit—which you are."

She's rambling. The apples of her cheeks have turned that pretty shade of pink again, and I smile at her for what feels like the hundredth time, despite having only met her hours ago. Elle just told me she thinks I'm sexy.

With a grin, I lead her over to the bar, refusing to move my hand from her back. I'm guessing, based on her reaction, she hasn't said this to many men in her life. Which is fine by me. I like being one of the special few.

"Can I get you something else to drink?" I smile at her as I tip my head close to hers. She's ditched her cake, and I have a feeling she's lost her appetite.

"God, alcohol sounds great right now. Yes."

"Something stronger than champagne?" I ask once we reach the bar.

Elle bites her lower lip, squinting as she thinks it over. "I'd better not. I'm not usually much of a drinker. I don't want to be hungover tomorrow."

"Probably a good plan, especially since it'll be a long day with the wedding and reception and all."

Elle's a good girl. I like that about her. It's refreshing. She's probably never stepped out of her comfort zone, or hell, even disobeyed a traffic signal in her entire life. And even though her ex is here treating her like shit, she's composed enough not to get shit-faced. It's classy, and I like that about her.

I signal the bartender and ask for another glass of champagne for her, and a tonic water with lime for me.

"What about you?" She tilts her head to the glass of tonic water the bartender sets in front of me. "Not a big drinker either?"

"Something like that." I don't tell her that I have a self-imposed one-drink maximum when I'm working. But being with Elle doesn't feel like working. Not even a little bit. And some small part of me knows that's dangerous.

Being here with Elle, mingling with the wedding guests, laughing, sharing a cocktail—it all feels completely natural. I don't have to fake having a good time when I'm with her. It's so rare for me to completely forget that I'm working. In fact, I don't think it's ever happened before.

It probably makes me sound like a pussy, but there's something satisfying about a woman enjoying me, my company—without me having to pretend to be something I'm not. It makes me feel appreciated and charming. And the way she's looking at me now, like I'm her knight in fucking shining armor after I saved her from her ex? Subconsciously, I like that a hell of a lot.

Part of me wishes we'd met under normal circumstances. Like at a bar, or a coffee shop, or a bookstore.

I imagine us bumping into each other and striking up a conversation. Within minutes, Elle would be laughing, her cheeks flushing pink. We'd exchange numbers, and I'd ask her out to dinner. It's been so long since I've been on a real date, one that doesn't involve a pre-set payment amount.

But of course, that's just a fantasy, because as soon as she found out what I did for a living, Elle's pretty little face would fall, and that would be the end of that. No one wants a boyfriend who sleeps with other women for a living.

Stupid, Nic.

It's dangerous to even fantasize about things like that. Elle won't ever be my girlfriend. I'm here to do a job, save her from her dipshit ex, collect my paycheck, and go the fuck home. Alone. End of story.

She enjoys her glass of bubbly, and when she's through, we mingle with a few of her relatives. Her ex takes off after a while, and she visibly relaxes once he's gone.

By the end of the night, Elle and I are leaning on the railing of the restaurant balcony overlooking a small man-made lake. It's a little corny—obviously a ploy to make the place seem more romantic—but between the moonlight and the slight breeze moving through her hair, even I have to admit that it's working.

"I had a great time tonight, Nic," Elle says, running her fingers over the black wrought iron. "When Christine told me she had a friend from college she wanted me to meet, I wasn't sure what to expect. But I definitely wasn't expecting someone like you."

That makes two of us.

I smile and place my hand gently over hers. "I

feel the same way."

Elle slowly brings her eyes to mine, the look in them a familiar one. Engaged and serious, but soft and inviting. She's giving me *the look*. The one that means she wants to kiss me.

A soft gust of wind blows her hair into her face, and I instinctively brush it away, tucking her coppery tresses behind her ear. Just as I'm about to lean in, my lips parted in anticipation, I stop myself.

What the fuck am I doing?

Sighing inside, I pull away and mutter something about the moon being beautiful tonight. The look on Elle's face is one of confusion mixed with disappointment, but she forces a small smile and nods.

It's a rule. My number-one rule, actually. I don't kiss on the mouth. Not on dates with clients.

This job won't last forever, and at some point, I'll have a serious girlfriend—hell, maybe even a wife. I won't be able to erase what I've done to make ends meet in this profession. But I do want to save *something* for the woman I end up with. Something special that hasn't been tainted by this job, and if a kiss is all that I can salvage, then so be it.

Although tainted isn't exactly the word I would use to describe what I imagine a kiss with Elle would be like.

"It's getting late," I say, watching the other guests trickle out of the restaurant below us. "Big day tomorrow. Can't have you staying up too late tonight."

Elle doesn't meet my gaze as she nods, then loops her arm through mine.

As I walk her to my car, she's quiet, probably still confused about why I stopped that kiss. I'd be lying if I didn't admit I'm a little confused and disappointed myself. This job isn't going the way I expected.

Twenty minutes later, I drop Elle off at her place. In the car, I asked her to walk me through the plan for tomorrow, and the air between us finally settled again.

By the time she climbed out of my car, we were both smiling and laughing, our connection having returned to easy and comfortable. This is exactly where the night needs to end if tomorrow is going to go well.

At home, I kick off my shoes and hang my dress clothes in the closet. The tux Case bought for me a couple years ago has been tossed onto my bed in a garment bag. He must have dropped it off while I was out. It's industry standard to have formal wear on hand, and he makes sure all of us guys look good. Hell, that's what we're paid for.

I pull my undershirt over my head and toss it into the hamper, then slip on a pair of athletic shorts before getting in bed. Although my line of work can be tiring, I'm surprised by how tired I am. Even when I don't have sex with a client, it can be mentally taxing, but it doesn't normally wipe me out like this.

I run my hand roughly over my face, pausing to rub my temples. It's Elle. Has to be. Something about her puts me on edge and relaxes me at the same time. We've only spent one evening together, and already I feel caught in an emotional push-and-pull that's totally new to me. And dangerous.

I have a job to do. That's that.

My phone buzzes on the bedside table, so I grab it and check the notification.

Well, think of the devil.

I open the text from Elle. It's a picture of two dresses laid out side by side on a bed, accompanied by a question.

Plum or silver?

I smile. Some part of me likes the fact that it's the night before the wedding, and she still hasn't decided what to wear. And it doesn't escape my notice that she's asking me instead of someone closer to her, like her mother or Christine.

I examine the two dresses closer, happily recalling every dip and curve of Elle's body and trying to imagine what it would look like in each one. I'm tempted to text back asking for pictures of her in each one, but I decide not to. Don't want to come across as too forward. Besides, my memory serves me just fine. But I do realize that both dresses seem to be fluttery and flowy, making me wonder if she's too self-conscious to wear something formfitting.

I frown at the thought. The woman is gorgeous. It's a fucking shame she doesn't know it.

Biting my lip, I send off my reply with a few swipes across my screen. It'll be my job to make sure she knows how good she looks tomorrow night.

As I settle into bed, tucking my arm beneath my pillow, a thought crosses my mind. I'm glad I have another day on this job, with this client. I'm glad tonight wasn't the last time I'll ever see Elle.

Chapter Five

Elle

I 'm just putting on my last swipe of mascara when my phone lets out a happy chirp. Nic is here to pick me up. Just seeing his name pop up on the screen makes butterflies fill my stomach.

I take one last look in the mirror. Satisfied with the way the plum-colored dress fits, hugging my cleavage and then flaring out, I grab my purse.

Last night went better than I ever could have imagined. As well as it went, I'm not sure if I should be offended that Nic didn't try to kiss me at the end of the night. Maybe he's just old-fashioned, or he doesn't want to make a move too soon and freak me out.

When I step outside, he's waiting for me by the car. His black tuxedo is perfectly tailored to accentuate his muscular body. As I lean in to give him a quick hug, I breathe him in. He smells so good— like leather and musk and something else I can't quite place.

"You look beautiful. Stunning, actually," he says as he pulls back to look at me again.

"You don't look so bad, either." I grin, staring into his chocolate-brown eyes.

"So, you ready for this?" he asks, cocking an eyebrow.

"Totally ready. But I don't know if you're ready for the waterworks." When he looks confused for a moment, I confess. "I always cry at weddings."

"I think that's sweet." He smiles, pulling open the car door for me.

I slap him playfully on the arm before I climb in. His car is a sleek black Tesla with a leather interior. I realize I never asked him what he does for work. He must be pretty successful to afford a car like this.

"What do you do for a living, by the way?" I ask as he climbs into the car next to me.

He stiffens for a second before shutting the door and starting the engine. "Finance," he says, then adds quickly, "It's not exciting."

I sense he's being short on purpose, so I decide to drop it. Maybe it stresses him out to discuss work in his free time. He definitely seems tense, but then I see his body relax and he smiles at me.

"My real dream is to work in real estate development," he says as he pulls away from the curb. "Building custom homes."

"That's amazing." I grin at him. "How'd you get interested in that?"

He shrugs. "I've always loved driving through nice neighborhoods and admiring the architecture. We didn't have much money growing up, and I guess it was always my dream to live in a big, beautiful house."

"I used to drag my parents to open houses in our neighborhood," I say. "Maybe we'll have to go to one together."

He glances at me, a smile playing on his full lips. "Maybe we will."

As Nic drives, I think about what he's just told me. The more I learn about him, the more interesting I find him. The fact that he grew up poor is a total shock—at first glance, you'd think he's the kind of guy who's breezed his way through life. But I admire that he's worked hard for his money.

When we pull up to the church, there's already a crowd. I lead Nic to the front where my mom is sitting. She pulls me into a big hug as soon as she sees me, and I can tell she's already on the verge of tears.

"Mom, the wedding hasn't even started yet." I laugh as she sniffles.

"My son is getting married," she says, swatting me on the arm. "I'll cry as much as I want to."

"Mom, this is Nic," I tell her, stepping aside so they can shake hands.

"Very nice to meet you," Nic says. "You've got some great kids."

"Of course they're great," she says, smirking at him. "I raised them."

We all laugh, and my mom gives me a look. I can tell she's going to grill me later about who Nic is and why I haven't told her about him.

As we take our seats, I turn to Nic and whisper, "Sorry I didn't warn you about my mom. She can be a little sassy."

"She's amazing." Nic grins at me. "I like a woman with her own opinion."

As the ceremony starts, I grab my mom's hand. I know she's going to totally lose it, and sure enough, within a minute, tears run down her face.

The ceremony is short and sweet. But when I see my brother gazing at Christine like she's his whole world, and listen to them repeat their vows, I start to cry too. I'm so happy for them; they truly are perfect for each other.

I'm sniveling like a baby, but I don't care. I'm so full of love for the both of them. And I'm secretly pleased they chose not to have a wedding party up there with them. Fewer people to witness my waterworks.

I try to wipe my tears away, but Nic pulls a tissue from his jacket and hands it to me.

"You brought tissues?" I ask, incredulous.

"I had a feeling you'd need them." He grins.

I stare at him, still blown away by his chiseled jaw and mesmerizing brown eyes. He's the complete package. Why is this man single? He must be a serial killer. I make a mental note to interrogate Christine about his lack of attachment later.

After the ceremony, everyone heads to the champagne reception, which is held in a pavilion overlooking the lake. As he drives, I can't stop glancing at Nic.

He handled meeting my mom so well. Sometimes, she can be a bit much when you don't know her, which could turn some people off. But she apparently didn't even faze him, which I'm grateful for.

Even the way he drives is sexy, his big strong hands placed firmly on the wheel. It's impossible not to think about how much I want his hands firmly placed on *me*.

When we arrive, Nic opens the door and helps me step out of the car. "Have I mentioned yet how amazing you look in that dress? It was definitely the right choice," he says, smiling at me as we walk toward the crowd.

I smile back at him, my heart pounding. I'm too aware of the way the dress hugs my curves, and the fact that it shows a little more cleavage than I'm comfortable with. Normally, I would have gone with a safer, more conservative dress, but something about Nic makes me want to break all my rules. Which is why I messaged him last night for his opinion, rather than reaching out to Christine or another friend who knows what my boundaries are.

"Then again, you probably would have looked stunning in either of them," he adds, looking me up and down.

A shiver runs through me. Wait until you see me with the dress off.

Biting my lip, I chastise myself. *Down, girl.*

It's only been an hour, and I'm more than ready to sleep with him. This is so not like me, but for once in my life, I'm ready to throw caution to the wind.

"Are you this smooth with all the ladies?" I ask when I see he's still watching me.

A shadow seems to pass over his face, but it happens so quickly, I start to doubt my own eyes and think I might have imagined it. Before I know it, the moment has passed, and he's grinning at me again, back to his normal self.

"I just enjoy giving compliments. Is that so wrong?" He raises one dark brow.

"No." I smirk at him as I grab two champagne flutes for us from a nearby server. "It's not wrong at all."

He watches me for a moment as we wander away from the party with our champagne, picking our way down the path to the lake.

"I like that you're not afraid to call me out, because there's plenty of guys who'll say whatever it takes to get what they want," he says finally, sipping his champagne. "There's also a lot of women who just tell me what they think I want to hear. But you're different."

"I guess I'm one of a kind," I say, half joking. I've never been great at accepting compliments. It's easier to deflect kind words with a joke.

"You are," he says, completely serious.

I look into his eyes for a moment, no longer smiling. We're standing close enough to touch, and I wonder if this is the moment he's finally going to kiss me. My heart is racing, and I lean forward with anticipation. But then he breaks eye contact and takes a step back.

What the hell?

"This is so beautiful," he says, walking to the edge of the water.

Floored, I stay back for a second. What just happened? It seemed like the perfect moment, and then it's like a switch flipped. I recover quickly and follow him to the water, trying not to let it get me down.

I know we have a connection; that's something I'm completely sure of. I just have to believe that he has a good reason for waiting to kiss me. But what is he waiting for?

As I join Nic, I take in the scene around us. Willow trees line the banks where water laps gently, and baby ducks swim nearby. The sun is about to set, lending everything a golden glow.

"I always loved feeding the ducks when I was little," I tell him. "I used to tell my parents I wanted to bring a leash so I could take one home." I grin at Nic, and he turns to me and laughs. "Luckily, I think they always knew I'd never be able to catch one to put a leash on it, but they humored me by letting me bring a leash."

"So you made your own rules, even as a kid." He laughs. "I like that."

I don't want to tell Nic that he's got me all wrong. I'm way more of a rule-following coward than he thinks I am, but I prefer seeing myself through his eyes. And for once, I'm determined to be that carefree, reckless woman he sees when he looks at me. The one who lives life to the fullest and does what she wants.

"I'm really glad I was able to be your date this weekend," he says, breaking the silence.

I turn to him. "I'm glad you came too."

Nic takes a step closer, bringing one strong arm around me. I have to force myself not to shiver with pleasure at the physical contact. My heart slams into my rib cage, and I take a deep breath to steady myself.

Glancing at him, I take in his strong jaw and tousled hair. I can picture running my hands through it and slipping my fingers into it during sex, especially while he has his face between my legs, and that thought causes my face to flush. The feel of his bicep against my shoulder sends heat racing through me, straight down to my lady parts. Just as I'm about to lure him into a bathroom somewhere to satisfy my out-of-control libido, we're interrupted by my mother.

"Here you are," she shouts to us, and Nic lets his arm drop away.

My shoulders are still warm from his touch, but I force myself to stop all thoughts of Nic. The last thing I need is for my mom to see how smitten I am with him.

"Christine and your brother are finished with the photos, and she's asking for you," Mom says, looking between Nic and me with a knowing smile.

"Okay, I'll be right there," I say quickly, before she can make any comments about us sneaking off together. I turn to Nic. "You'll be okay for a few minutes?"

"Of course. Go," he says warmly.

I follow my mom to the bridal suite where Christine is waiting. As soon as I see her, I pull her into a hug and burst into tears again. Then we're both crying and laughing at the same time.

"We're ridiculous," she says, pulling back.

"Wait, stop crying. You're going to ruin your makeup." Sniffling, I wipe smudged mascara from beneath her eyes.

"Oh, it's way too late for that," she says, and we laugh again. "Now, can you get me out of this thing?"

After I help to bustle her dress and remove her veil for the reception, we each pop a breath mint. As Christine touches up her makeup. I figure it's now or never to grill her about Nic.

"So, why haven't you ever talked about Nic before now?" I ask casually. "I want to know more about him."

Christine pauses for a second. "I told you, it's because you were with Jeremy. It wasn't like I could spark up a conversation with you about him in front of your current boyfriend."

"I know. He's just such an amazing guy, and being with him is making me realize how much of my life I wasted on Jeremy." I almost start to tear up all over again, but this time from sadness and not from the excitement of seeing Christine and my brother getting married. "I just want to know his story."

"Come on, no more tears. Let's go have some fun and dance the night away with our arm candy," Christine says, obviously changing the subject to a happier topic. "They're waiting on us, I'm sure."

We head out of the suite and back into the ballroom together. But as far as I'm concerned, this conversation is far from over.

"Give me something, Christine, like what else is there to know about him? I mean, is he a good guy?" I ask, pushing her. She's usually happy to gossip about new guys in my life, so I don't know why she's choosing this moment to act coy.

"He's really sweet and fun, Elle, but don't read too much into anything he says. He's really more of a casual-dating kind of guy."

I pause, taken aback. Nic definitely doesn't strike me as a strictly casual guy. Last night, he wouldn't even kiss me, and I was basically throwing myself at him. Maybe he's holding back because he's friends with Christine, and he doesn't want to risk their friendship by having a one-night stand with her sister-in-law. Lucky for him, a quick fling is exactly what I need right now to pull me out of this funk I'm in.

I shrug at Christine. "Casual works for me. Tonight I just want to have fun, get drunk, and maybe even do something reckless . . . like get laid." Rebound sex could be exactly what the doctor ordered to get me past this hiccup in my love life.

I spot Nic across the room and smile at him, a shiver running through me at the thought of possibly going home with him. I tear my gaze away from him and notice Christine is looking between the two of us. She's not smiling, and she's gone totally pale.

"I don't think that's a good idea," she says finally. "He's great to have as your date to make Jeremy jealous, but I think you should leave it at that."

She's acting so strange about this, and I can't figure out why. Am I missing something?

"What's gotten into you?" I ask. "You're constantly telling me how I need to get out more and cut loose, and now I want to and you're against it."

Christine bites her lip. What could be so bad about Nic that she's trying this hard to keep me away from him?

"Look, I just saw you go through all this heartbreak with Jeremy, and I think you should focus on you right now," she says, putting her hands on my shoulders. "Promise me you won't sleep with him?"

What the hell?

I really have no idea what's going on. So what if Nic was a ladies' man in college? If I'm okay with it, Christine should be okay with it too. Why even set me up with someone she didn't want me to pursue?

Nothing makes sense, and I want to keep pushing her, but I also don't want to make a huge deal of this on her special day, so I decide to just drop it.

"Okay, I won't sleep with him," I tell her, and she smiles, clearly relieved.

I feel bad, because I totally don't mean what I just said. I've never lied to Christine before, but if she can't give me a good reason not to sleep with Nic, then I don't know why I should listen to her. And if things get heated between the two of us later . . . I can't argue with chemistry, right?

Trying to shake off my guilt, I rejoin Nic. He's talking to a group of my elderly relatives, and they're all laughing at something he's just said.

I can't stop the grin from spreading across my face. On top of everything else, he's amazing with my family. A lot of guys would be intimidated to meet a woman's entire extended family on the second date, but Nic is taking it all in stride. And it doesn't hurt that he looks tantalizingly sexy all dressed up in his tux.

Sorry, Christine. I can't let her get into my head.

Nic looks so good, it's going to take a lot more than some dirty laundry from his past to stop me from ending the night in his bed.

Chapter Six

Nic

Elle and I are seated at a table near the front, a little to the right of the wedding party's table. The servers are milling around us, taking away our salad plates and replacing them with entrées. Elle has the chicken option, while it looks like Christine picked the beef for me.

Perfect.

"Can I get you something to drink?" the server asks as he sets my plate in front of me.

I glance at my now-empty champagne flute from earlier and shake my head. My one-drink rule is going to be even more crucial now that I know I clearly have a hard time controlling myself around Elle.

And who can blame me? She's unbearably sexy

in that dress. I should have picked the other one. Not that it would have made that big a difference because she's got curves in all the right places, and neither of those dresses would have left much to my imagination. The creamy swell of her ample breasts is visible above the neckline, and while the hem is modest and drops to her knees, I know exactly the kind of hourglass figure she's hiding beneath those layers of chiffon.

Down, boy.

"What about you, miss?" The server turns to Elle, who cocks her head to the side for a moment, looking at me as she tries to decide.

"Don't let me stop you from having a good time," I say, flashing her a casual smile.

"You're really going to make me drink alone?" She swats my arm with the back of her hand, her expression playful.

My arm tingles where she hit it, not because it hurt, but because I'm suddenly so aware of every time our bodies touch. When I position my body toward her, our knees brush, and I allow my fingers to graze hers.

"Everyone here is drinking like there's no tomorrow. I'd hardly call that drinking alone. Besides, I need to keep my wits about me around you, beautiful."

A blush spreads across her cheeks, moving down her neck and dangerously close to her cleavage. It takes every ounce of my self-control not to take a good look at just how close it gets.

Elle raises a challenging eyebrow at me before turning to flash a smile at the waiter. "I'll have another glass of champagne, please."

The waiter nods and walks away, moving around the table to take drink orders from other guests.

"After all . . ." Elle looks me in the eye and crosses her legs so her calf rubs fully against my leg. "This is a celebration, isn't it?"

Fuck. This is going to be much more difficult than I thought.

After dinner, the maid of honor and best man give their speeches, and there's hardly a dry eye in the room. When I notice Elle dabbing at her eyes with the back of her hand, I give her another tissue from my jacket pocket and she laughs, shaking her head at how prepared I am.

What can I say? I'm a professional.

After the toasts, the dancing begins, and I pull Elle out on the dance floor with me. Not that she needs much persuading. She had another glass of champagne with her dessert, and she's clearly feeling it.

The DJ plays a few good upbeat songs, and the two of us find our rhythm easily, our bodies moving in sync. It's perfect. Too perfect. And that can only mean amazing things about what our bodies could do with no clothes on.

Just as the playlist slows down, the mood shifting to something more sensual, Christine walks over and clamps her hand firmly on my forearm.

"Can I steal him for a sec?" she asks Elle. Her tone is light and cheery, but her grip on my arm tells me something is wrong.

"Just be sure to bring him back in one piece," Elle replies with a wink.

"I promise. Besides, my *husband* was wanting to dance with his sister, so I thought this was the perfect opportunity for us to swap."

Christine forces a laugh and jerks me away. I smile calmly to Elle and mentally prepare myself for whatever new element is about to be added to this job. Good thing I stuck to my one-drink rule.

She leads me to a small hallway around the corner from the dance floor, where the volume is a bit lower and the lighting slightly dimmer. Christine finally releases my arm, facing me straight on, her shoulders squared with mine. Although she's still in her pretty white wedding gown, she definitely looks ready for battle. Before she even opens her mouth to speak, her body language says it all. She's pissed.

"Elle wants to sleep with you tonight," Christine says, her tone warning.

Well, shit. I raise my eyebrows. "Okay . . ."

"I just want to make it clear that that's not what I'm paying for. Plus, I'm sure it costs extra."

She's not wrong. Sex does cost extra. Part of me wants to respond with something witty, but it's clear she's upset, and I'm not about to be the man who makes a woman feel worse. Especially on her wedding day.

"Things won't get that far. You don't need to worry, Christine. I'm a professional." I keep my tone calm and relaxed, trying to exude as much confidence as possible.

But on the inside? I have no idea how I'll manage to say no to Elle. Not when all I really want to do is to pull her into this hallway and pound her into a wall.

Suddenly, it hits me. Elle told Christine she wants to sleep with me. That's the only reason we're having this conversation right now.

A small smile crosses my lips. So she does want me. *Bad*. It's not like she's the first woman in the world to do so. But Elle's different. For some reason, knowing she's itching to jump my bones means a whole lot more than the other women who pay for it.

Christine seems to watch my thought process cross my face, and her eyes narrow. "Things are going a little *too* well, if you ask me," she mutters. She crosses her arms and stands up straighter, challenging me.

"Sorry I'm so good at my job." I chuckle.

Her face darkens. "Yes, but Elle doesn't know it's a job, asshole. This is real for her. You have to be careful. I swear to God, if you hurt her, I will end you."

With that, Christine turns and marches away, her wedding dress rustling with the movement. The venom in her voice lingers in the air around me. And it stings. Worse than I thought it would.

Of course, I knew going into this that Elle was just a job. But from the moment I met her, everything felt different. It never felt like work. This wasn't me on my best, most dazzling behavior trying to impress some rich cougar. This was me just being myself, having fun with a girl close to my own age.

And now that I know she's attracted to me, that she wants me too? Everything is even more complicated.

It's against company policy to sleep with clients who aren't paying for it. Mixing business and pleasure is a huge no-no in our line of work. It's normal for things to get confusing for our clients— they're the ones who forget they're paying for it while it happens. But for me? The fact that I'm working needs to always be at the forefront of my mind.

I have to say no to Elle. It's the right thing to do. But turning down sex with a beautiful woman, the kind of woman who makes me wish I'd met her under any other circumstance, who reminds me of the kind of man I want to be one day? Yeah, that's not going to be an easy thing to do. I haven't had sex just for pleasure in a long time. Probably at least a year. God, that's fucking depressing to think about.

But I definitely can't take Elle to bed without her knowing the score.

I return to the dance floor to find Elle dancing with her mom. We make eye contact and she smiles, her whole face lighting up at the sight of me. Guess she isn't going to make this easy on me.

I make my way toward her, slip my hand around her waist, and lean closer to bring my lips to her ear. "Can I get you something to drink?"

She nods, taking my hand in hers and swaying her hips. We dance our way over to the bar, where I grab her another glass of champagne, and we continue dancing.

If I thought Elle was sexy just standing around and talking, dancing with her is a whole other ball game. The way she moves her hips drives me crazy, and it doesn't take long for her to start rubbing up against me, her arms swaying above her head while she moves her ass over the front of my pants.

Hello, hard dick.

Not helpful.

Slowly, she turns to face me, our mouths only inches apart. Her big blue eyes travel over my face, landing on my lips, and she places her hands on my chest. I need to strategically adjust what's happening in my pants before I give myself away.

"Want to get some air?" Her breath is hot on my skin.

I nod and take her hand, leading her to the balcony. I guess balconies are becoming our thing.

"So, when you were little, did you imagine yourself going into this line of work?"

Her question is innocent enough, but for a moment, I freeze. Then I remember—she thinks I work in finance. My shoulders relax, and I flash her a smile.

"Not exactly. When I was five, I wanted to be a lion tamer. Probably not very realistic."

A grin stretches across her face. "Were you afraid of lions when you were five?"

"*The Lion King* was my favorite movie, so I guess not."

We laugh, and Elle leans toward me, our bodies dangerously close to touching. It wouldn't take much to close the distance between us, one of us to make first contact. Just a few more inches, and we'll be kissing.

But I can't. I have rules for a reason.

"What about you? What did you want to be when you grow up?"

She sighs and leans against the railing, pushing a hand through her long auburn hair. "I've always wanted to be a lawyer," she says, looking over the railing at the landscape below. "I went through law school and everything, but never had the guts to take the bar exam. It's too daunting. And I can't bear the thought of failing it. So yeah, I'm just a paralegal."

My stomach clenches. Of course she's brilliant. It makes me like her even more. "I think you'd make a great lawyer. You've already won me over."

Whoa, whoa, whoa. Get a hold of yourself, Nic.

A small smile passes over her lips. "I don't know about that. But thank you. It's nice to hear you say that."

She looks up at me then, her eyes wide and searching. I'm lost in them, lost in their deep, blue expanse, when she opens her mouth and says something I didn't expect to hear.

"Where did you come from?"

The wistfulness in her voice catches me off

guard, almost matched by the yearning in her eyes. They're boring into me, hitting me in a place I haven't been hit in a long time—right square in the chest.

Suddenly, everything else fades away. My job, Christine, Case, my rules. None of that matters anymore. I know what I want.

Fuck the rules.

I bring my hand to her face, cradling her cheek in my palm, and pull her toward me. Her skin is so soft, I can hardly stand it. Elle tilts her head as I bring my lips to hers, and for a moment, I hold her there, our lips only a bit apart, so I can feel her breath on my skin. Her eyes close just as our mouths meet, and she practically melts in my arms.

The moment our lips touch, everything seems right. She has the softest lips I've ever tasted, and when they part, I sweep my tongue inside. With growing confidence, I increase the pressure, sealing my mouth over hers. Elle makes a low murmured sound of approval, and her hands move to my biceps.

It's in that moment that I lose my shit. Keeping one hand on her chin, I press the other against her lower back and use it to bring her even closer. I'm sure she can feel what she's done to me, but in that moment, I don't care.

Her full breasts are crushed against my chest, and I can feel her heart hammering fast. The sensation of her tongue tasting mine makes me feel so light-headed and filled with need, I can't help the husky noise that rumbles in the back of my throat. Amazed, I pull back to meet her eyes.

She's fucking perfect.

This woman is perfect.

Everything about the past two nights has been perfect.

And I'm totally fucked.

Chapter Seven

Elle

Finally, I think, leaning into Nic. His full lips are pressed against mine, and my heart is beating so hard, I can barely breathe.

His kiss is tender, yet demanding. Soft, yet firm. Bossy, yet so accommodating. If this kiss is any indication of how good he is in bed, I'm in for a wild ride.

I don't know if it's all the champagne I drank earlier, but I'm drunk on the feeling of Nic's body close to mine.

He presses his hand to a spot on my lower back, just above my butt, and I let out a little moan. Heat floods my body, going straight between my legs. His tongue teases mine, slowly at first and then more insistently, and a shiver runs through me.

The sounds of the reception have all faded away, and any doubts that Christine planted in my head are gone. When he pulls back, all I can think is that I want to feel whatever I just felt forever.

We stare at each other for a few moments, breathing heavily.

"That was . . ." His voice trails off.

"Yeah," I whisper, staring into his eyes.

Nic lets out a sigh. "I didn't expect anything like this to happen." He sounds almost apologetic.

"We're both adults." I smile, putting a hand on his arm. "You don't have to look so guilty."

He gives me a strange look before smiling back at me, then nods, his eyes hazy with desire. "You're right."

I touch his cheek and pull him in for another kiss. His hand caresses my shoulder, and everywhere he touches feels electrified. I'm desperate for him to touch me anywhere. Suddenly, kisses aren't enough. I want more.

"Should we get out of here?" I ask, pulling back. I'm not normally so brazen, but what the hell? A sexy man is into me. If the situation in his pants is any indication, I'd say he's into me big-time. Emphasis on the *big*.

Nic doesn't say anything at first, just stares intensely into my eyes. He looks almost conflicted as he leans back and studies me.

Suddenly, my heart skips a beat—did I misjudge this whole thing? I'm never this forward with guys, and I hope I'm not the only one feeling like my world was just rocked by our kiss.

"Are you sure you're ready to go?" he asks finally, and relief floods through me.

"Yes." I grab his hand and tug him toward the exit. I walk quickly, glancing around the room to check if Christine can see us. Luckily, she's on the dance floor with my brother and some of our friends, and doesn't notice us leaving.

I pull Nic out the door without saying goodbye to my family. I don't think I could stand the thought of having multiple conversations wishing my relatives farewell when all I can think about is ripping Nic's tux off. Besides, I'll see them all at brunch in the morning.

When we reach Nic's car, he pulls out his keys and our arms brush. He turns to look at me, and my stomach flips as I take in his strong chest and muscular biceps. I can still remember the way those firm biceps felt beneath his jacket.

He takes a step toward me, so close we're almost touching, his dark eyes searching mine. Then he takes another step and presses up against me, pinning me against the car.

Nic puts his hands on either side of me and touches his lips to mine again. His tongue strokes mine as he kisses me more urgently, and his hands slide down my hips and up my back.

My breasts press against his strong chest, my nipples hard underneath the fabric of my dress. I slide my hands up his biceps, feeling his muscles straining underneath his tux. I feel like I'm losing all control, and I'm just about ready to let him strip my dress off right here in the parking lot when he pulls back. He's breathing heavily as he moves me to the side and pulls open the car door.

"We should get going," he says, his voice thick and deep.

I nod, my chest heaving. At this point, I'm ready to go old school and have sex in his back seat, anything to have this man inside me as quickly as possible. He's looking at me with so much lust in his eyes, I'm sure it must mirror my own.

"So," he says, running his hand through his

hair. "What's your favorite flavor of ice cream?"

I blink at him for a moment and then laugh. "Ice cream?"

"Yeah. I'm trying to distract myself. So, what's your favorite flavor?" He smirks, stepping away from me and moving to the driver's side.

I slide into the car. My legs feel weak, and I'm light-headed from the rush of his body pressing into mine, but I decide to play along.

"Anything with chocolate and peanut butter will make me happy," I tell him.

He nods, then starts the car and pulls out of the lot. "Good choice. Mine's butter pecan."

I glance at him out of the corner of my eye. "Really? Butter pecan?"

He looks over at me. "What's wrong with butter pecan?"

"It's fine," I say, smirking at him. "If you're my grandfather."

Nic laughs. "I guess I'm just an old-fashioned guy."

If the night so far is any indication, I'd say he's anything but old-fashioned.

He navigates through the streets quickly, and I can tell he wants to get to my place as quickly as I do. Whatever trick he's trying to use to keep my mind off of how much I want him isn't working. I guess I'm really embracing my resolution to stop following the rules all the time, because I feel bold in a way I never have before.

I watch Nic's hands on the wheel for a moment, then take in his profile. His strong jaw is even more pronounced in profile, highlighted in the dim lights of the car, and I can still feel the roughness of his facial hair from our kiss. Unable to resist, I slide a hand onto Nic's thigh as he drives.

"Hey, I thought we were trying to distract ourselves," he says, swallowing hard. "What's your favorite season?"

"Hmm . . ." I move my hand up his thigh. "Fall. You?"

I glance at the bulge in his pants, and if it's any indication, I'd say he's very well endowed. I can tell he's trying to focus on the road, but his chest is moving up and down rapidly.

"You're going to make me crash," he says finally.

I give him a sly smile and move my hand even

higher up his leg.

"Jesus." He huffs out a breath and presses the gas harder, then glances at me. "I might have underestimated you. You're going to be a handful, aren't you?"

"You have no idea." I grin, stroking his thigh.

Something about being with Nic is freeing; I'm feeling totally uninhibited for the first time in a long time. Just touching his thigh has me so hot and bothered, I can barely stand it. If he can make me feel this way without even touching me, I can only imagine what he can do with all our clothes off.

Luckily, the reception venue was close to my place, and Nic makes it there in record time. My legs still feel weak with desire, and I try to focus on opening my front door without dropping my keys.

As I turn on the lights, I mentally congratulate myself for having the foresight to clean my apartment before I left this morning. As Nic takes in the space, I look around the room, trying to see it through his eyes.

With a car like he has, I can only imagine he lives in one of the amazing high-rises downtown. I don't make a ton of money, so my place is pretty modest, but I've done what I can to make it comfortable.

"Nice place," he says, turning to me with a smile.

"It's okay." I shrug, setting my purse on the side table. "I want to move soon."

"I'm serious. I really like it," he says, grinning at me. "It feels like a real home, you know? I've gotten too used to my bachelor pad, but it's just that, a place to sleep."

I smile, and for a moment I wonder how many women he brings to that bachelor pad.

Shaking my head, I chastise myself. Why am I even thinking about that now? And who cares, anyway? This whole night is about me having fun, casual sex, and the number of women Nic has slept with isn't any of my business.

"Do you want something to drink?" I head toward the kitchen.

"I'm okay," he says, moving to the side table where I keep old family photos.

Shit. I should have hidden those.

"Is this you?" he asks, his tone amused as he holds up a framed photo of me as a kid. It was during a phase where I wanted to be a magician, and I was in a full tux and top hat, holding up a stuffed rabbit.

Fucking awesome.

I move across the room and grab the photo, heat rising into my cheeks. "Can we save the trip down memory lane for another time?" I don't think having Nic see photos of me in my awkward pre-teen phase is the right way to kick off our one-night stand.

"It's cute." He grins at me. "So, you went to law school and can pull a rabbit out of a hat. Any other hidden talents?"

Wouldn't you like to know?

I set the photo facedown on the table and grab Nic's hand, tugging him toward me. I don't want him to think I'm cute; I want him to fuck my brains out. And I think we've waited long enough.

I step closer until our bodies are almost touching, and he gazes down on me, his dark eyes finding mine. He's freaking delicious—certainly unlike any man I've ever dated. Seeing him standing next to Jeremy was almost comical. Where my ex is all gangly limbs and an ill-fitting suit, Nic commands attention with his height and broad shoulders. It's like he was cut from a *GQ Magazine*.

I swallow, suddenly unsure about how he's feeling, and wish I didn't have quite so much to drink tonight. Doubt creeps into the edges of my brain. Nic hasn't pounced on me, hasn't made a move yet, but he did kiss me back . . .

"Are you sure you want this?" I ask tentatively.

He takes a step closer and places my palm against the front of his pants. "Does that feel like I'm unsure, Elle?"

My throat closes. Holy shit, the man is rock hard. *For me.* The thought is dizzying.

Damn, I need this so much. I didn't know it until this exact moment, but something about his undivided attention, his focus on me, is somehow repairing the destruction Jeremy left behind. Nic knows what he wants, and somehow that's me. His attention feels so good, I may just black out before we get to the main event.

Taking two steps forward, he backs me up against the wall, still staring into my eyes. He moves his hands up my arms, trailing his fingers gently over my bare skin. I shiver, totally consumed by him—his dark, smoldering eyes and the feel of his hands on me.

When he reaches my shoulders, he moves his hands lower, trailing light touches along my collarbone. I let out a little moan, arching my back toward him, desperate for his hands on my breasts. He smirks as he takes his hands off of me, still staring into my eyes, and I squirm with desire. He's teasing me, and it's totally working.

"You're so sexy," he whispers, placing his hands on my hips and kissing along my neck.

I can feel how wet I am already just from this little bit of attention. There's an ache between my legs for him, and I'm practically shaking with need. I wrap my arms around him and pull him in for another kiss.

He tugs my hips tight against him as his tongue enters my mouth hungrily. I can feel the large bulge in his pants pressing into me, and it just ramps up my desire. My heart pounds against his, and he presses himself even closer so that I'm pushed completely against the wall. His hands move to my breasts, cupping them through my dress, and he brushes his fingertips over my hardening nipples.

I'm so overwhelmed, and when I open my eyes, the room is spinning. I don't know if it's Nic or the champagne or both, but suddenly, I feel like I need to take a breather.

"Wait," I say, breathing hard as I pull back. As his eyes search mine, I swallow and push him away. "I'll be right back."

I walk to the bathroom, thinking I just need to splash some water on my face. I glance back at Nic before I shut the bathroom door, and he's still breathing heavily, watching me with that same conflicted look on his face from earlier.

Alone in the bathroom, I take a deep breath. I don't know why Nic looks so conflicted, or why Christine tried to stop me from doing this. All I know is that no other guy has ever made me feel this way before, and I don't think I could stop now . . . even if I wanted to.

Chapter Eight

Nic

What the fuck am I doing?

Standing in the middle of Elle's bedroom like an idiot, that's what.

I can't believe I came inside. I should have just dropped her off and gone back to my place. But now here I am, more turned on than I have been in months, and waiting for the girl I want to come back from the bathroom so we can finish what we started the moment we got through the door. It doesn't take a genius to figure out where that action is heading.

What was I thinking?

Pushing my hands through my hair, I start pacing the room.

Maybe there's still a way out of this. My dick

won't be happy about it, but I can tell Elle I'd rather take things slow. Give her a kiss good-bye and be done with it. Once she's done in the bathroom, I'll gather all the self-control I have and shut this down. It's the only option.

As I pass by the bathroom door, I can hear Elle coughing. The sound doesn't stop, and when I realize she's retching, my stomach drops. This is my fault. She told me she was a lightweight. Told me that she never drank very much. I should have kept a closer eye on her, made sure she didn't drink too much.

I rush through the door and find her hunched over the toilet, and the helpless look on her face makes my heart ache. With one hand, I pull her hair away from her face, holding it loosely between her shoulder blades. I use the other to rub the straining muscles on her back, tense from vomiting.

Elle takes one look at me and starts sobbing, tears streaming down her face. "Oh my God, Nic, I'm so sorry. I should have been better than this. It's just that I, like, never drink," she says between breaths.

"Don't apologize. This shit happens to everyone every once in a while," I reply, brushing a few stray hairs away from her face.

She sniffles and nods, mustering a weak smile before flushing the toilet and rising to her feet. I help her to the sink, where she brushes her teeth.

When she's done, I carry her back to her room and seat her on the edge of her bed. Once she's settled, I go to the kitchen and bring her a tall glass of water and a bottle of aspirin, placing them on her bedside table.

Her watchful gaze follows me, and I'm relieved that at least my straining erection has died down.

"Can I help you change?" I ask.

Elle nods, remaining quiet.

I unzip the back of her gown, and she stands so it falls to the floor in a puddle around her bare feet. I keep my eyes trained on her red-painted toe-nails to avoid looking at the curve of her hips or the creaminess of her full breasts.

"What do you like to sleep in?" I ask, my voice thick.

"Just a T-shirt, please. Second drawer."

I cross the room to her dresser and open the drawer she's indicated. I pull out a soft gray T-shirt and hand it to her.

After tucking her in, I leave one last kiss on her forehead and tell her good night.

As I drive home in silence, my mind spins with everything that happened between Elle and me tonight. How could I have been so stupid? I'm getting lazy. Careless. I'm supposed to be a professional, but tonight I felt like anything but. This isn't like me. And I need to get my shit together—fast.

Once home, I strip off my tuxedo and hang it up, then brush my teeth, eager to get some shut-eye. Despite how many of my rules I broke by kissing Elle on the mouth and going home with her, at least things didn't go any further than that. Because as much as I want to believe that I'm the kind of man who has an endless supply of self-control and discipline, if Elle had wanted to fuck me, there's no way I would have been able to say no.

If tonight confirmed anything for me, it's that Elle hits all my weak spots, even the ones I didn't know I had.

I grab my phone before tucking in for the night and shoot Elle a quick text to check in on her. I doubt she'll even text me back tonight—she's probably passed out—but I like the idea of her waking up knowing I was thinking about her.

Fuck, I really am screwed with this one.

At work the next day, I have my usual meeting with Case to go over my clients for that week and make sure everything is running smoothly. We've been going over business as usual for half an hour when he leans back in his chair and raises an eyebrow at me.

"Hey, how did it go with that chick who didn't know you're being paid to date her?"

I sigh and push my hand through my hair. Not exactly the direction I wanted this meeting to go. "It was fine. You know how it is—another day, another client. She didn't seem to catch on."

Case nods but doesn't reply right away, eyeing me for a few awkward seconds. "Was the client happy with how it went?"

My mind flashes to Christine pulling me aside at the wedding, basically yelling at me for being too good at my job. She totally got in my head about everything between Elle and me, and now that I think about it more, I think her yelling at me was partly why I decided to go home with Elle after all, rules be damned.

But I can't let Case know any of that.

I shrug. "I think the lying part freaked her out a little by the end. But hey, she paid in full, so no complaints here."

He eyes me again, then crosses his arms. "Something's different with this chick, man. It's written all over your face. What, did you break one of your precious rules?"

I grit my teeth, instantly furious with how well Case knows me.

Asshole.

"Nothing happened. Now, if you're done grilling me, I have work to do." Pushing my chair back, I stand to leave.

Case smirks at me and cocks his head to the side. "All right, whatever you say. Just don't ever tell me I'm not the kind of boss who's here to listen."

I roll my eyes and march toward the living room.

I know he's just trying to help, but Case is the last person I want to talk to about all this. For as much as he likes to work me to the bone—pun intended—he's always trying to get me to loosen up a little bit, have more fun on the job. Too bad I'm learning really quickly just how much trouble a little fun can get you.

I check the time. Four thirty. Time for me to pick up my Sunday regular.

Every Sunday I take Esther, my oldest client, to dinner at her country club. It's not sexual, by any means—not that I'm here to judge anyone for their age preferences. I just pretend to be her charming and successful grandson to impress her snooty old friends. Probably the easiest money I make in this job, especially since I see these rich pricks enough to know just what to say to get Esther in good with them, and make them jealous because none of their grandchildren give them the time of day.

Today I'm dressed in a cream-colored linen suit and a pale gingham checked button-down. I look every bit like a spoiled, wealthy heir. Basically, I fit right in.

When I enter the dining room, Esther is already there, dressed in a baby-blue sundress, reaching her aged-spotted hands toward me as a smile overtakes her mouth.

"There's my handsome grandson," she says, a little more loudly than necessary.

I chuckle and return her warm embrace. "Good to see you. How was your week, Gram?"

She winks at me, one heavy-lidded blue eye dancing with knowing mischief. "Just peachy."

"Excellent. Now, are you ready for dinner?"

I offer her my arm and we stroll into the dining room. She waves to a few of her friends from her book club as we head to our usual table.

Once we're seated, a tuxedo-clad server delivers two goblets of ice-cold water and a basket of warm bread. Esther doesn't drink, and so neither do I when I'm with her. We each order the steak-and-lobster special before the server scurries away. Sometimes, I really love the perks of this job.

Most days, we keep dinner conversations light. The weather, the latest drama in her bridge group, that kind of stuff. For as annoying as I find the country club crowd, I've grown to like Esther. She's a little less judgmental than the rest of them, even if she buys into some of their elitist bullshit.

Which is why I'm really not prepared when she asks me about my love life.

"So, Nicky, are you dating anyone?"

Just my fucking luck.

I plaster a fake smile on my face while I decide how to answer. Normally, I don't divulge anything personal to my clients, but Esther's different. I know she's only asking because she genuinely cares, but after Case's questioning earlier, I'm not up for another conversation about Elle.

Still, Esther is someone I really trust, despite being a client, so I decide to be honest with her.

"Not right now."

"You're almost thirty. You're going to want to settle down soon, aren't you?"

My face falls at the mention of my age. *Way to hit a man right where it hurts.*

"First, I'm not *almost* thirty. I'm only twenty-eight."

She purses her lips. "Close enough. When I was your age, I'd been married for six years and had three children already."

I take a sip of my water, stalling for time. "Of course I want to settle down. Eventually. But it's difficult for someone like me to date. Who would want a boyfriend who *entertains* other women for a living?"

Esther smiles, reaching across the table to pat my hand. "You're a good boy, Nicky. I knew it from the first time we met. Why do you think I keep scheduling these dinners?"

I smile at her, but I don't take her words to heart. Not really. Part of me is appreciative of her support, but a larger part of me knows she's just being nice.

"It's easy to be polite and charming when you're getting paid to do it."

She squeezes my hand, her soft, wrinkled fingers looping around my palm. "Don't lose faith. The right girl is out there. There's someone for you just around the corner. I know it."

I smile and nod, squeezing her hand back before letting go.

Esther means well, but she must know I'm right—what girl in her right mind would want to get involved with me? Even though I'm a male escort, I still want to find love someday.

But that's not a topic I want to think about right now. So I turn the tables on Esther and ask how her latest crochet project is coming along. She smiles, and thankfully lets the topic drop.

When I get home later that night, Esther's words are still ringing in my head. I always thought the idea of soul mates was stupid, that there was no way there was really someone out there for everyone. That people who bought into that shit were chumps.

But after everything that's happened, meeting Elle and having my whole world shaken to its core?

I don't know what to think anymore.

Chapter Nine

Elle

I glance at my phone, checking for any texts. Nothing. I let out a huff and turn back to my laptop.

I'm trying to focus on work, and it's not going very well. The lawyer I work for just landed a big client and has assigned me a ton of research for the case. Not that I'm complaining; I'm happy for anything that can distract me from the total mortification I've been wallowing in after this weekend.

Standing up from my desk, I stretch, hoping that a quick break will help me refocus on the piles of documents in front of me.

My head still feels fuzzy from this weekend. I can't believe what was supposed to be my carefree, casual hookup ended with me throwing up for an hour. I don't know what got into me; I can't even remember the last time I drank that much. I blame it on my attraction to Nic. I got caught up in the rush of being with him, and just lost control of myself.

God, I wonder what Nic must think about me.

We're way too old to be getting that sloppy. He probably thinks I'm a hot mess and never wants to see me again. I haven't heard from him since that night, and I was too ashamed to reach out to him yesterday. I know I need to apologize if I want any chance of things being okay between us, so I decide to send him a text.

Biting my lip, I pull out my phone.

```
Are you free to meet for coffee
this week?
```

After pressing SEND, I squeeze my eyes closed, then put the phone facedown. I need to focus on work, and staring at my phone won't make him respond any faster.

After a few minutes, I can't resist anymore and check my messages. To my surprise, Nic has already responded.

I pull up the text, preparing myself for rejection.

I let out a sigh of relief. After exchanging a few texts, we decide to meet Thursday afternoon since my boss will be out of the office for the day, and I want to keep this meeting casual, not like a date. I'm already feeling a huge weight lift off of me.

I should have known he wouldn't hold a grudge over this. He's not like most of the other guys I've dated who would be pissed at me for giving them blue balls. I smile to myself as I get back to my research, finally ready to dive into my huge workload.

It seems like the more I learn about Nic, the more amazing he is. I just hope it's not too late to salvage our connection from this past weekend.

Frustrated, I stare into my closet. I've tried on about fifteen different outfits, and none of them seem right. I need an outfit that says I'm put together, and not a hot mess. Something that also says I'm interested in more. It might be just a quick mid-afternoon coffee date, but I still want to look good and yet not break the dress code at work. Finally, I settle on casual black skinny jeans and a pink blouse.

It's ridiculous to be this nervous . . . it's not like Nic has never seen me before. But I still haven't officially apologized for last weekend, and I'm not sure how he'll react. It's possible that after seeing me as a drunk, crying mess bent over a toilet while I'm dry heaving, he just wants to be friends, but I hope that's not the case.

As I slip out of the office that afternoon and drive to the café, I plan what I'm going to say. I just want to make sure he knows I usually act like a responsible, trustworthy adult and not a teenage sorority girl. My nerves kick in as I walk in and pick a table. I'm first, so I order a latte and settle into my seat, trying not to stare at the door as I wait. I'm scrolling through social media, hoping to distract myself, when the door opens and Nic walks in.

I have to take a deep breath because it feels like all the air just left the room. Nic looks as gorgeous as ever in jeans and a black T-shirt.

When he sees me, he smiles, and my heart swells. How does he look just as good in casual clothes as he does in a suit?

I stand to give him a quick hug, and when our bodies touch, heat shoots through me and straight between my legs. I swallow, wondering if he can tell what I'm thinking. I didn't expect to still have such a strong reaction to him, but he looks so good, I'm ready to forget the coffee and go back to my place for a do-over.

"It's good to see you again," he says as we pull back from the hug. His lips are turned up in a half smile, and his eyes are alight with playful satisfaction at seeing me.

Relief floods through me, and I grin up at him. "You too," I manage to say, still smiling.

I try not to stare as he orders at the counter, and I'm not the only one. Women all around the café are looking at him. And who can blame them when he looks like he just walked off the pages of *GQ*?

He's barely back at the table when I launch into my apology.

"So, look, about the other night," I say, fidgeting with my cup. "I'm really sorry. I never, ever get that drunk."

Nic holds up a hand and smiles. "There's no need to apologize. Like I said, it happens to everyone." He takes a sip of his coffee, then smiles warmly at me. "Trust me, I've been there more times than I'd like to admit."

"Well, I just wanted to let you know I don't usually take guys home and immediately start throwing up." I grin back at him, so blown away by how open and forgiving he is that I can't keep the smile off my face. Or maybe it's just that it's so nice to see him again.

"It wasn't my typical experience with a woman," he says, smirking. "But that's what I like about you. I never know what to expect."

We laugh, and I do an internal happy dance. I'm so relieved we can still joke around with each other.

"How's work going?" I ask, grateful that we can move on to normal conversation. "I know you're probably really busy, so thanks for meeting me."

I can't figure out why he's dressed in jeans and a T-shirt rather than a suit. I know he works in finance and it's not yet quitting time on a Thursday. Then I think that maybe his firm is really casual, less stuffy than the norm like ours is. Maybe it's one of those internet startups run by a twenty-two-year-old or something.

"Work is fine," he says.

I get the sense again that he doesn't want to discuss work, so I don't ask any more questions. He's being so sweet that my heart is skipping. I've never dated a guy like this, someone who is so thoughtful and forgiving all the time. It's refreshing, and I could definitely get used to it.

"How's paralegal life?" he asks, interrupting my thoughts. "Have you signed up to take the bar yet?"

"It's busy," I say, filling him in on the big new client we signed. "And no bar exam yet. But I'll get there. Hopefully someday."

Being around Nic really does make me feel like anything is possible. And with my new go-for-it attitude, I actually might sign up to take test.

"Well, whenever you do take it, I know you're going to ace it," he says. "After knowing you for five minutes, I could already tell how smart and driven you are. You probably have a much higher IQ than most of the lawyers at your firm, and most of the women I've dated, for that matter."

I chuckle at his compliment, shaking my head. "And how many women is that?" I ask playfully, raising an eyebrow.

His face falls for a second, and I mentally slap myself. Why did I even say that?

"I'm totally joking," I say quickly, trying to recover. "Your love life is none of my business."

I smile, trying to reassure him. I don't want to let on that Christine told me about his playboy past, but I'm afraid I just made it obvious. Maybe it's something he's touchy about, or maybe he just doesn't like to share so many personal details. Either way, I can tell I struck a chord.

His expression goes back to neutral. "I can say that honestly, none of them compare to you." He looks at me with the same intensity from Saturday night, his eyes searching mine. "Not even close."

I shake my head. "Are your pickup lines always this bad?"

Nic laughs, and God, do I love the sound of that. It's deep and rich and genuine. "Probably. But most girls don't call me out on them."

He looks at me then . . . really looks at me, like he's seeing me for the first time. My belly flips.

I stare back into his eyes, lost in the moment. My heart is pounding, and I want to reach across the table and pull him against me.

Finally, I break eye contact with him and look away. I almost forgot we were in a public place. Taking a sip of my latte, I try not to think about all the things I wish we had done on Saturday night.

"So, how's Christine enjoying married life?" he asks, saving me from my thoughts.

"They're on their honeymoon in Hawaii right now. She just sent me pictures of them hiking near a volcano." I pull out my phone to show him the photos.

"They seem really happy," he says, smiling. "Good for them."

"You sound surprised," I say, raising an eyebrow. "Are you one of those guys who thinks marriage is a scam?"

He shakes his head. "Not at all. I'm looking forward to domestic life, actually. Two kids, maybe a couple of dogs."

I grin at him. "White picket fence?"

"Exactly," he says, laughing.

It's all too easy for me to picture myself cuddling up with Nic in a cute house in the suburbs.

Jesus, Elle, slow down.

I'm usually not like this when I first meet a guy, but something about Nic is so enticing—hell, so comfortable—that I can't help but imagine what a future with him would be like.

"So, tell me more about this dream of yours," I say. "Building custom homes. When exactly are you going to start your business?"

He sighs. "We'll see. It's a pretty big undertaking."

I nod. "How about a pact? If I take the bar exam, you have to start your business."

He takes a breath. "That's a pretty serious commitment." He watches me for a moment before holding out a hand. "Deal."

We shake hands on it, and I ask him more about his plans for the business. The more he tells me, the more I can tell how passionate he is about this.

It's so easy to be around him, joking and talking about our futures, that I don't even realize how much time has passed until a barista comes to our table and asks if we'd like another round.

"Oh my God, has it really been an hour?" Looking up from my watch, I frown. "I have some work to catch up on before tomorrow."

I don't want to leave, but I know I have to get home to my laptop so I can finish the work I missed this afternoon. As much as I'd like to keep spending time with Nic, I can't just blow off my responsibilities. He nods, looking disappointed.

"Let me walk you to your car," he says, standing.

Outside is a perfect fall day. The sun is dipping toward the horizon, and there's a cool breeze in the air. The leaves have all changed to bright oranges and reds, and they crunch under our feet as we walk through the parking lot.

"This was really fun," I say once we get to my car, turning to face Nic. "Thanks for being so understanding about this weekend."

"You really need to stop worrying about that," he says. "But it's cute that you were so nervous."

I slap his arm playfully, grinning. "I wasn't nervous."

He smiles at me, and when our eyes meet, he takes a step closer, his dark eyes latching onto mine. Then he lifts my chin with his fingers before gently pressing his lips to mine. I lean in, wrapping my arms around his shoulders, and he puts an arm around my waist, pulling me in closer.

I close my eyes, giving in to the feel of his body pressing against mine. He's kissing me softly, and the moment is so sweet, I want it to last forever.

My stomach flips as he trails his fingers along my lower back, and I grip the back of his head with my hand. When he pulls back, I want to reach for him again, but I force myself to take a step back.

I realize I want Nic to know how I'm feeling. Usually, I'm too afraid to discuss my emotions with a guy I don't know very well, but I'm trying to be brave, and it's now or never. I take a deep breath.

"Look, I don't know if you're looking for anything serious right now, and it's totally fine if you're not, but I have fun when I'm with you." I say it quickly, before I lose my nerve. I watch Nic, trying to gauge his reaction.

"I wasn't expecting you," he says, his eyes searching mine. "I don't know what I'm looking for, but I agree, I like being with you. Should we see where it goes?" His expression is relaxed, happy, his mouth quirking up in a half smile as he says this.

My face breaks into a grin, and I feel like jumping in the air and cheering. Instead, I give him a tight nod.

As I drive home and then make myself an early dinner, I'm practically giddy. Once I've eaten and before I get to work, I decide to text Christine.

```
Tell   me   everything   you   know
about Nic.
```

Since Nic and I didn't have sex, I technically kept my promise to Christine from Saturday night. If she asks, I won't even have to lie.

Besides, I need to know more about him before this goes any further, because after today, I'm determined to get Nic in bed to finish what we started.

Chapter Ten

Nic

My alarm blares, waking me from the most restless night's sleep I've had in a long time. I roll over and glare at the clock. Six thirty. Time to get up, brush my teeth, hit the gym, shower, and head to work. Just a day like any other.

Except no part of me wants to do any of that. The idea of entertaining any woman who's not Elle makes me want to hit something.

I sit up with a groan and stretch my limbs. My head is screaming like I pounded half a bottle of Scotch last night, and my entire body aches. I'm not normally a stressed-out person. But lately it feels like every muscle in my body is on edge, tense and ready for a fight that may or may not be coming.

My phone chimes again, reminding me it's time to leave for the gym. If I don't make it out the door on time, my schedule for the day will be totally thrown off. Case isn't happy when I show up late for work, but if I'm being honest with myself? I don't give a rat's ass about how Case feels right now.

After stumbling into the kitchen, I make myself a cup of coffee, rubbing my temples to soothe the headache. I blend my usual protein shake, adding an extra handful of wheatgrass for good measure. I'm trying to gear myself up for work when it hits me—I should just cancel. There's no way I'll be useful to anyone if I feel this shitty.

I dial Case's number and bring my phone to my face, wedging it between my shoulder and ear as I pour my smoothie into a glass.

"Hey, dude, this is an early call for you. What's going on?"

At least Case sounds like he's in a good mood. For now.

"Hey, I just wanted to let you know I can't come in today," I say, keeping my voice low and gravelly. "I think I caught a twenty-four-hour bug or something, and I don't want to get anyone else sick."

It's not a complete lie. I do feel like shit. It just might be more psychosomatic than I'm letting on.

"What the fuck, Nic? I had you slated to meet with two different clients later, plus a pre-screening interview this morning. How the fuck am I supposed to get one of the guys to cover on such short notice?"

"If you want me to infect all those nice women, I can push through it. I'm sure Jay from legal will be thrilled to hear you made that call."

Case swears under his breath, and I can practically hear him pacing around his office. Jay is a buddy of his, and also an attorney who's gotten Case's company out of a jam a time or two.

"I don't know what's going on with you, Nic, but you know I count on you. Please tell me this has nothing to do with that girl from the other night."

Low blow.

"It's nothing like that, I swear. I just need a day to make sure I'm not contagious."

"Fine. But I'll need you to pick up a few more clients this weekend. Maybe even a double shift."

I sigh and pinch the bridge of my nose. This conversation really isn't helping the feeling like my head is about to explode. "Sure, whatever you need. Listen, I have to go. I think I'm about to up-chuck this smoothie."

"Yeah, whatever, asshole. Thanks for royally screwing me over today."

Thanks, dude. Hope you have a good day too.

I hang up and toss my phone on the couch with more force than necessary. I know I should feel worse about lying to my boss, but I have too many other things to worry about to let that weigh me down.

Well . . . one other thing.

Elle.

Our coffee date yesterday was incredible. Part of me was hoping that seeing her outside of work, during the day, would break the spell. That we would meet up and the spark would be gone, the magic of a wedding weekend faded.

But the moment I saw her sitting at that table, a smile spreading across her face as she saw me, I knew that would never happen. Our connection wasn't about the circumstances, although I'm sure the fact that she thought I was an old friend of a friend helped. But despite all that, the meet-up went way better than I thought it would. And that just makes everything more complicated.

I pop a couple of ibuprofen and down a glass of water. I have to kick whatever's going on with me. I'm not normally like this, not the kind of guy who gets taken out by a fucking headache. And definitely not the kind of guy to get hung up on anyone, especially not a client.

Honestly, I wish feelings were as easy to get rid of as headaches. Then at least I could take a couple of pills and be done with it.

I like her, actually *like* her, and it's a position I haven't found myself in in a very long time. Years. It's new, and honestly, it's refreshing.

I decide to hit the gym anyway, even if I'm not heading to work later. Running will probably make the headache worse, but I think swimming a few laps might help. Something about the water always makes me feel a little better.

I throw a pair of trunks into my gym bag and hop in the car. A workout will be good. Clear my head a little.

But even with my body gliding through the

cold pool water, I still can't shake these thoughts about Elle. It's like she's worked her way into my bloodstream, and it feels like no matter what I do, I can't stop thinking about her. There's something oddly cathartic and ironic about this situation—and Elle, if I think about it.

Maybe the problem is simpler than I originally thought. Maybe the fact that I'm keeping myself from her is making this whole situation seem a lot more exciting than it really is. I spend time with beautiful women who want to fuck me all the time. The only thing that makes this one any different is that I won't let myself have her.

So maybe that's what I have to do. Ask Elle out, sleep with her, and be done with it. I should know better than anyone that anticipation makes cocks harder and panties wetter.

That's what I have to do, then. Set up a proper date, one I'm not getting paid for. If it's not work, then all bets are off. No rules, no policies to keep in mind. Just two adults acting on the natural chemistry between them. And once the mystery of what Elle Alexander is like in bed is broken, I'll be free of her, free to move on with my life and go back to business as usual.

Problem solved.

At this epiphany, I stop swimming and climb from the pool to towel off. Right then, I grab my phone and consider shooting off another text to Case. I don't like the idea that he's pissed at me. Yeah, he's my boss, but he's also a friend.

Unsure what I'd even say, I stuff my phone into my bag and head to the locker room to get dressed. Once I'm changed and on the drive back home, my mind drifts back to when I first started working for Case.

It's been a crazy six years, and he's always trusted me, always believed in me—maybe even when he shouldn't have.

I remember the week I started working at Allure. I didn't know it at the time, but the motherfucker set me up to find out how talented I was (or not) in the bedroom. I should have seen right through this, but I was twenty-two and horny, and basically, I fell for it hook, line, and sinker.

Case, Ryder, and I went out to a nightclub together one night. It was a typical Friday for us, and there was nothing out of the ordinary—except for the fact I'd just started working for him.

We each ordered a whiskey and sipped them while Case and Ryder entertained me with stories about some of the women they'd met in this line of work, and all the crazy shit that was in store for me.

As we talked, I noticed an attractive woman at the bar watching me, bringing her straw to her lips and giving me bedroom eyes. At first, I was hesitant to leave my new boss to go approach her, but Case only laughed and shoved my shoulder, telling me to get my ass over there. He said he intended to keep me so busy that this might be the last time I had sex with a civilian for a while.

The woman was beautiful, about ten years older than me, and said she was in town only for the night on business. It was my first time being with an older woman, and there was a lot I liked about it. She knew what she wanted in the bedroom, was confident and charming, and we had a great night together in her hotel room.

The next morning, Gia, who turned out to be a friend of Case's, reported every vivid detail of our encounter to my new boss.

"You suck at sex, dude," he said when I entered his office the next morning.

"That's not what your mom said," I joked.

"Gia emailed me this morning with a very colorful critique."

My eyebrows darted up. "What are you talking about?"

I'd had a couple of steady girlfriends and a handful of casual encounters with women I'd met on dating apps over the years, and as far as I knew, not a one had ever complained about my performance.

He only smirked. "You didn't think I'd send you out there without some field-testing first, did you? Can't have some lousy lay ruining the reputation I've built my company on."

"You talked to Gia?" I blurted, sinking into the leather chair in front of his desk.

He poked a finger at his screen and scrolled through a rather lengthy email. "You thrust too fast, your kisses were sloppy, and your foreplay needs to last longer. Oh, and the vagina is sensitive, dude. You don't just ram your fingers or tongue right in there. You've got to tease her, build up to it, make her want it first."

"Seriously? She said all that?"

He nodded. His face was impassive, and he didn't look the least bit surprised.

I had no idea what this meant. I remember being worried that Case was going to fire me. And just generally feeling like shit because I thought she'd had a good time.

"I thought we had fun," I murmured.

"Actually, she did have fun." He pointed to his screen again, scanning the bottom paragraph as he read it out loud to me. "She said you were fun and playful, and had amazing potential with a little bit of coaching. Said you had a big dick too, though it's not a detail I wanted to know."

"Okay . . . so, what do we do?"

Case smiled and folded his hands on his desk. "Sex happens to be my specialty. I'll teach you everything you need to know, and then with your new knowledge, you'll go rock Gia's world. Once she says you pass, then I can start setting you up with clients."

I nodded, feeling more than a little sheepish. "Okay. Sounds like a plan."

Case leaned back in his chair. "First, you need to understand how women think about sex. It's a lot different from the way you or I probably think about it. If you really want her to enjoy herself, you need to pleasure her mind first, and then her body."

I thought I got what he was saying. For me, sex was physical. I saw a hot girl; I wanted to take her to bed. Boom. End of story. At least, that was how twenty-two-year-old me operated.

When it came to Elle, clearly, I have a lot more self-control than I ever realized.

Case launched into a lecture, and I tried to absorb every word. "It's important to spend more time on foreplay than you think you need. It helps to tease her before, get her wet and build anticipation. And as I mentioned, you want to start slow. The clitoris has eight thousand more nerve endings than a penis, so you want to use gentle pressure until she's ready for more."

Rather than feeling uncomfortable about the conversation, I recall leaning forward in interest. I knew that Case knew what the hell he was talking about, and he wasn't trying to talk down to me. I could tell he legitimately wanted to help me.

"How will I know she's ready for more?" I asked.

"You'll be reading her reactions. Everything will be about her pleasure—not yours. You'll listen to her cues and watch for her responses, and then you can build up from there."

We spent three hours going over every detail that would make me, ultimately, a much better lover. From little things, like when you're fucking a girl in missionary position, not to just balance on top of her with your forearms on either side of her shoulders. Instead, you should place one hand on the back of her neck and the other under her shoulder, increasing your skin-to-skin contact. Then we moved on to bigger things, like making sure you build trust and rapport with her to make her feel as comfortable as possible before you get into bed together.

More than just learning about sexual techniques and positions, Case taught me a lot about how to talk to women, how to use open-ended questions and make the conversations about them—their hopes, dreams, motivations, and things they love to do.

"And Nic?"

"Yeah?"

"Don't worry. No one's ever passed Gia's test on the first try."

His words made me feel slightly better.

The following day, I met with her for another encounter, this one a very hands-on instructional meeting, and I passed with flying colors. After that, I began meeting with clients, and have been hard at work ever since. Pun intended, I guess.

I don't recall ever taking a day off unexpectedly like this in the last six years, except for that time I had food poisoning. And as soon as I work Elle out of my system, I know I'll be right back to fucking my way through Case's clientele, making us both very rich men.

Chapter Eleven

Elle

"You look like you had such an amazing time," I say as Christine swipes through her photos of Hawaii. It's the first time I've seen her since the wedding, and she's absolutely glowing. We're at my favorite wine bar downtown, and after half a glass of merlot, I'm feeling sentimental.

"I don't know if it's the tan or the marriage, but something you're doing is working for you," I say, grinning at her. I'm so happy for her and my brother. They really are the perfect couple.

She laughs, putting her phone away. "It's probably the relief of making it through the wedding without anything going horribly wrong." She takes a sip of her chardonnay before continuing. "What have you been up to? I feel like I haven't seen you in forever."

I fill her in on everything that's been going on with work. Secretly, I've been dying to ask her more about Nic, but I don't want to seem too eager. When I texted her asking her to tell me more about him, she seemed hesitant and didn't say much, but I'm not letting her off the hook that easily. If she didn't want me to ask about Nic, she should have known better than to set us up. Especially when she knows he's basically the sexiest, sweetest guy alive. I mean, seriously.

"I also saw Nic again," I admit after I've finished telling her about work. I give her a sheepish look, anticipating her judgment.

"Elle!" she says, as if she's admonishing me for something.

"What?" I shake my head. "I don't get it. You're the one who set us up."

"To make Jeremy jealous," she says, giving me a serious look. "Not to start dating. Don't tell me you slept with him."

"No, I didn't sleep with him." I sigh. "We just got coffee and talked. It was very PG; you would have been so proud of me, *Mom.*" I decide not to tell her that after the wedding, I was ready to ride him like a stallion before I got too drunk. "Look, whatever happened in college that makes you think he's not dating material isn't true anymore. He's changed. He's been a total gentleman with me."

"People don't change, Elle, trust me," she says, taking another sip of her wine.

I'm still baffled by how weird she's being about this whole thing. Like she thinks he's slimy. I've never heard her talk about someone this way, even people she doesn't like, and supposedly she and Nic were close. But then why did she set me up with him on a blind date? It's strange.

"Did you guys have a thing or something?" I have a loose theory that Christine and Nic hooked up in college, and now she feels weird about the thought of us getting together.

"What? No way. I'm just being protective. I don't want to see you get hurt again, that's all, and we both know that rebound men are never keepers." She stares at me intently, and despite how strange she's acting, I can tell she genuinely does care.

Before I can say anything else, my phone vibrates. It's a text from Nic, and my heart jumps at the sight of his name on my screen.

Are you free for dinner this
week?

"I'm going to be fine. Also, he just asked me out to dinner," I say, unable to keep the smile off my face, even in front of Christine.

When I show her the text, she looks horrified. I hold myself back from rolling my eyes.

"Christine, whatever douchey things Nic did in college are way in the past. Most college kids sow their wild oats during that time, right? And then they grow up to be normal people who get married and have children. Trust me, he's not like that anymore. If he were, don't you think he'd have tried to do more than just kiss me by now?"

"Please just be careful with this." She puts a hand on mine, looking into my eyes. "I can't tell you who to date, but just know that I'm warning you about this guy. I don't want you to end up with a broken heart."

"I am being careful," I say, frustration creeping into my voice. "When am I not careful? And why are you so sure I'll end up with a broken heart?"

Christine sighs and looks down at her hands. "I'm not sure; I'm just worried. But you're an adult, and I respect that. You can make your own decisions."

Damn right I can.

"He's a good guy, I promise. I know you've known him longer, but you haven't seen him in a long time. He's not a player, or an asshole, or anything like that. He's really sweet and supportive."

I don't tell her about his encouragement with the bar exam, or the sweet compliments he offered when Jeremy said I was too curvy. I have a feeling she'd only find a way to condemn them as being less than genuine.

Christine stares at me for a few moments without saying anything while she finishes her drink.

Not wanting to get into an argument with my friend and now sister-in-law, I decide to change the subject. We spend the next little while making plans to go to the farmers' market next weekend, and chat about a new chick flick we'd both like to go see.

After I finish my drink, I head home. I wait until after I leave Christine to accept Nic's invite. The truth is I'm more excited about this dinner date than I've been about anything in a long time.

```
I'd love to. Just tell me when and
                              where.
```

As I wait for his response, I decide not to mention Nic to Christine anymore. She clearly has some hang-ups about him, and until things get serious between him and me, there's no reason to argue about it. The last thing I need is her bad attitude clouding my time with Nic.

She's only a couple of years older than me, but she's acting like I'm her daughter. I'm perfectly capable of deciding who's a good person and who isn't all on my own, and I don't need her lecturing me.

Nic responds as I pull into my driveway, and my heart leaps again.

```
Saturday night, my place. I'll
cook for you.
```

I smile to myself as I step inside my apartment and start making my dinner. So I'll finally get to see where Nic lives, and if things go the way I hope they will, the night will be ending with more than just dessert.

Chapter Twelve

Nic

Tomatoes, onions, red wine, bay leaves . . .
what the hell am I forgetting?

I've scanned my pantry twenty times now,
racking my brain to make sure I'm not missing any
ingredients for my date with Elle tonight. Not that
that's really possible. I've already made three sepa-
rate grocery runs, just to be safe.

I don't normally cook for other people. Not
ever, really. I cook for myself all the time, but
it's never been a skill I've wanted to use to woo a
woman. Hell, I don't woo women at all . . . at least,
not in my personal life.

But from the moment I decided to take Elle
on a proper date, I knew it had to be special. And
cooking for someone—in my own home, no less—
is definitely not something I've ever done for a

woman before. But when the idea popped into my head, I knew it was perfect.

My place looks better now than it has for months, that's for sure. I'm no slob, but when no one is around to see it, I don't stay quite as on top of my scrubbing and dusting as I should. Until today, that is. I spent at least four hours deep cleaning every inch of my apartment. And I have to admit, it cleans up pretty damn good.

I lift the lid slightly on the large pot simmering on the stove. My mouth waters at the aroma, and I can't help but smile at the thought of Elle walking through my door and doing the same. Half the reason I decided to cook for her was to impress her with my domestic charm. But the other half of the reason? No part of me wants to take Elle in public and share her with other people. All I want is to have her here in my space, just the two of us.

Pecorino. That's what I'm forgetting. I quickly open my fridge and find a small wedge of the hard, pale cheese sitting in a drawer. Thank God I stay so true to my Italian roots.

A knock on the door makes my stomach drop. She's here.

I can't tell if I'm excited or nervous. But my

heart is hammering away, and my insides feel like someone twisted them with a fork.

Her effect on me is totally out of the ordinary—yet so damn invigorating at the same time. It's been a long-ass time since I've felt anything other than a professional duty to a woman, and I realize I've missed that feeling more than I care to admit.

Before opening the door, I check my reflection in the hallway mirror, pushing a few stray hairs back into place. It's go time.

When I open the door, my heart skips a beat. Elle's gorgeous. Somehow even more gorgeous than the last time I saw her.

She smiles and self-consciously tucks her hair behind her ear. "I'm so glad this is you. I was worried I'd be banging on the wrong door." She chuckles, a slight blush creeping over her chest.

I drink in the sight of her, my mouth twitching with a smile. She's beautiful. Real. Adorable as fuck.

"Well, I'm glad you found me," I say, leaning in and placing a kiss on her cheek. I usher her inside, guiding her to the kitchen with my hand resting against the small of her back.

Elle's blue eyes widen as she takes in the cityscape view from the back wall of windows. "This place is amazing. Your line of work must pay really well, doesn't it? Maybe I need to rethink my law aspirations and go into finance," she says, and a small chuckle escapes those gorgeous lips.

My own smile falters for a second. My "finance" job isn't exactly the reminder I need at this moment.

"Here, let me take your purse."

For a second, I consider putting it in my bedroom like I would at a party. But ending the night by retrieving her purse from my bed would only lead to one thing. I don't want her to feel pressured to do anything she's not ready for, and I don't want to tempt myself even further. So I place her purse on the couch and return to the kitchen to check on the sauce.

I find Elle leaning against my granite countertop and admiring the view, her position showing off her supple curves. My pulse is racing, and I'm suddenly aware of how nervous I am in her presence.

I haven't gotten this worked up over a woman in years. What the fuck is going on with me? This date was supposed to help quell these feelings, not make them worse.

"Can I get you something to drink?"

Her gaze travels to me, the corner of her mouth lifting into a half smile. How does her every move manage to be sexy?

"That would be lovely."

I pull a couple of glasses down from the shelf and pour us each a sparkling water with a slice of lemon. Elle laughs, covering her face with her hands and shaking her head.

"I'm never going to live that night down, am I?"

I hand her a glass, and we clink glasses before taking a sip.

"That night was my fault. And I'm not making the mistake of overserving you again. Seeing you in so much discomfort and knowing I could have stopped it from happening . . . not my proudest moment."

"Are you kidding? I'm the lightweight who should have known better than to keep downing glass after glass of champagne."

"We'll call it a tie, then," I say, making my way around the island to stand next to her, our arms lightly brushing.

Elle turns to me and raises her glass for a toast, and I raise mine to join her.

"Cheers. To getting to know each other better," she says, her eyes sparkling in the candlelight.

"And to new beginnings," I add.

Our eyes lock as our glasses clink, and we each take a sip. Elle smiles at my addition, but the words feel more serious to me. I know she doesn't understand their weight for me, but I mean them. Something about this woman makes me want to turn over a new leaf. Even if that means taking a massive pay cut for a few months while I find a different line of work.

"So, the sauce needs to simmer for another twenty minutes or so. Why don't you take a seat by the windows, and I'll grab us some bread with olive oil?"

"Sounds perfect."

Elle settles into one of the plush chairs by the windows while I slice a few pieces of fresh, rustic Italian bread. Pouring the oil onto a small dish, I watch her admire the view for the second time this evening. My breath catches when I look at her.

Get a fucking grip, man.

Honestly, I'm starting to think it's a miracle she can't read me like an open book. Otherwise, I'd be eating out of the palm of her hand, even though I'm normally the one who has that effect on people.

I join her by the windows, setting the bread and oil on the small round table between us.

Our conversation flows easily, just like it did when we met for coffee. All the nerves weighing me down when Elle first got here slowly fade away. Being in her presence still puts me on edge, but talking with her reminds me how natural our connection is.

I don't have to pretend when I'm with her. And given what I do for a living, that makes her feel like a cool drink of water on the hottest day of the year. I can just be myself.

"So, Nic," Elle says after a brief pause in the conversation, leaning toward me. "Long term, where do you see yourself? Like, if money didn't matter, if nothing mattered except what you wanted to do, what would you do?"

The question takes me by surprise. Not that anything with Elle should surprise me anymore. Of course she knows just which question to ask to bring my walls down.

"Long term? I mean, I do want to settle down one day, even if that seems impossible with my job right now. Because my hours are so crazy," I quickly add. I don't think Elle suspects anything about the truth of what I do, but I'm not about to take any chances of that knowledge slipping out.

"Okay, so, say you do settle down. Do you want to stay in this job forever, or is there something else you want to do?"

I chuckle. If she only knew. "I'd definitely be doing something different."

I've already told her about my dream, but this time, I elaborate, telling her about my favorite types of architecture and the classes I've taken at the community college. I look up to find Elle staring at me, a soft smile on her pretty lips. Her expression is a mix of sympathy and admiration. It makes me feel amazing and embarrassed at the same time.

Sighing, I run my hand over my face. "Sorry for the monologue."

Way to kill the fucking mood, Nic.

But Elle reaches out and takes my hand in hers. "Don't apologize. Thank you for sharing. That's a really beautiful dream, and I hope you're able to make it come true one day."

We lock eyes, the warmth of the connection between us radiating to my toes. This time it's Elle who looks away first, shaking her head and chuckling softly.

"Just like me and the bar exam, I guess. Only I think my dream is a little more hopeless."

I run my thumb over her knuckles. "Don't say that. You'll take the bar one day, when you're ready. I know you'd make an incredible lawyer."

She snorts. "You're sweet. But at this point, I'm starting to think I'm going to need to hire someone to take the bar for me. I can't even think about signing up for that thing without getting all queasy."

I squeeze her hand and decide to drop the subject. The last thing I need is to make her ill for the second time on one of our dates.

"Well then, let's turn your attention to something a little less nausea-inducing. Tell me something about yourself that might surprise me."

Elle smiles and tosses a glossy lock of her auburn hair over her shoulder. "Well, that depends. What do you want to know?" she asks, her big blue eyes trained on mine.

More than I'd like to admit.

My mouth twists into a grin, and I lean toward her. "Just about everything."

"In that case . . ."

She begins telling me a story about the time she almost killed her class hamster in second grade, and by the end of it, the two of us are practically rolling on the floor laughing. We take turns exchanging stories from when we were young, each one more bizarre and endearing than the last.

My sides are starting to hurt from laughing so much. I can't believe how comfortable things are with her, how amazing this date is already going, and we haven't even started eating yet. There's no way I'm letting this girl go, not when every bone in my body is screaming that I'll never find anyone like her ever again.

But when Elle finds out the truth about what Christine hired me to do—will she still be here laughing with me? Or will she go home, wishing she'd never met me in the first place?

Chapter Thirteen

Elle

"I'm just about finished with this," Nic says, stirring a large pot on the stove. "You can head out to the terrace and I'll bring it out for you."

"You're such an amazing host." I smile at him.

He looks so comfortable and domestic in his state-of-the-art kitchen. Tonight he's dressed casually in jeans and a long-sleeved T-shirt that stretches across his broad shoulders and firm biceps in a way that makes my stomach dance with excitement.

So far, the night has gone beyond my expectations. When Nic said he wanted to cook for me, I figured it would be something out of a box. But if the smells coming from the pot he's stirring are any indication, he knows his way around the kitchen.

"This is just the beginning," he says, winking at me.

I laugh and wander out of the kitchen and through the living room, making my way onto the terrace. I figured Nic would have a nice place, but I didn't know it would be like this. He lives in a two-story penthouse in a high-rise downtown, with a view that goes on for miles.

Sipping my water, I take in the sparkling lights of the city. It's a perfect fall evening. The sun hasn't quite set yet, hanging just above the horizon and casting a golden glow over the skyscrapers.

The terrace itself is straight out of a romance novel. Nic has hung up string lights across the space, and has set a bistro table for two with flow-ers and a few candles. I grin to myself, thinking he's probably the only guy in the world who would be thoughtful enough to set a table this way.

In fact, his whole apartment is anything but the bachelor pad I would have guessed it to be. Nic has taken the time to hang art on the walls and his furniture actually goes together, unlike most guys I know who just throw a random assortment of couches into a room. He even has a few house-plants. He's either more of a homemaker than I thought, or he found a really good decorator. I'd think the latter, but somehow I know this is all Nic's doing.

My thoughts are interrupted by the terrace door sliding open. A few seconds later, Nic walks out holding two plates of pasta. He sets one down in front of me, and I breathe in the smell.

"It's gnocchi with a wild boar ragout," he says, settling into his seat.

"Wild boar?" I raise an eyebrow. "I didn't even know you could get that around here."

"I know a guy." He smirks.

I grin before taking my first bite. My eyes widen as I chew.

"Mmm," I say after swallowing, and look at Nic in shock. "You made this? It's so good. Is this homemade gnocchi?"

"Of course." He laughs. "You think a true Italian like me would serve you that packaged stuff? You deserve better than that."

I take another bite, trying to hold back a groan. It's so good, it's like an orgasm in my mouth. As I watch Nic take a bite, his strong jaw flexing as he chews, I can only hope it's not the only orgasm I'll be experiencing tonight.

"So, you figured I'm the kind of guy who orders takeout and tries to pass it off as his own cooking?" he asks, smirking.

"That's what every other guy I've dated has done. So, yeah, pretty much." I laugh. "How did you learn to make this?"

"I've always loved cooking," he says after taking a sip of his water. "My grandmother loved to cook and so does my mother, and I spent a lot of time in the kitchen with them when I was younger."

"Are you really Italian?" I ask.

He nods. "My name is actually Nicco, but no one calls me that except for my mother."

Once again, I'm blown away by Nic. Everything about this date is so romantic—the candlelight, the city views, and the amazing food. And not to mention Nic himself, who looks about as good as his pasta tastes.

His dark, messy hair is blowing gently in the breeze. His biceps flex as he runs a hand through his hair, and I bite my lip. I can tell he hits the gym more than the average guy, and I can't stop myself from imagining him putting those muscles to use in the bedroom. An image of him lifting me up against a wall during a hot make-out session flashes through my mind, and I feel my face heat up.

"Have you told Christine that we've been hanging out?" he asks, bringing me back to reality. He says it casually, but I sense something urgent in his tone.

"I haven't had much of a chance to talk to her," I say, then swallow. "Mostly just about the wedding and her honeymoon."

I hate lying, but I'm definitely not going to tell him what she said about him. Or that she's been practically begging me to stop seeing him.

"Makes sense." He smiles and nods, seeming relieved.

I can't shake the feeling that there's something those two aren't telling me, but I try to forget about it. I'm probably just paranoid because of everything Christine has said about him.

"So, what do you do in your free time? Besides cook gourmet meals and put together romantic dinners." I smile, wanting him to go along with changing the subject. The less we talk about Christine, the better, in my opinion. I don't need the reminder of her warnings about Nic ruining an otherwise perfect evening.

He laughs. "I love spending time outdoors, camping and hiking. I haven't traveled much, but I want to. We could never afford it growing up, and now that I actually have money, I don't have the time."

"I would love to travel more. I wanted to study abroad in college, but I chickened out."

"So, you've never been out of the country either?" he asks.

I shake my head. "If you could leave right now, where would you go?"

"I definitely would love to visit Italy. My family is from Florence, and I've always wanted to do a backpacking trip through Europe." He laughs. "But I might be too old for that now."

"No way, you're never too old to travel," I say, taking another bite of gnocchi. "That sounds perfect to me."

"Should we make another pact?" He gives me a playful smile. "That we'll travel to Europe within the next year?"

I grin back. "Let's do it."

The thought of sipping wine in a vineyard in Italy or lying on a beach in the south of France with

Nic is way too tempting. The idea of Nic in a bathing suit alone is making me feel hot and bothered.

It's so easy to picture a future with him, and I hope I'm not getting ahead of myself. I'm always so careful with my feelings, and suddenly with Nic, I'm throwing caution to the wind. I just hope our connection is as real as I think it is.

As we finish the last of our food, a cool fall breeze blows by, making me shiver.

"Should we head inside? It gets a little breezy up here," Nic says, standing to clear our plates.

I follow him back inside, where he gestures for me to sit on the couch as he takes our plates into the kitchen. When he comes back, he's holding two plates of dessert.

I raise an eyebrow. "You can bake too? I think I might be in love with you."

As soon as I say it, my face turns red. I may be totally smitten with him, but I don't want to come on too strong, too fast.

Luckily, he just laughs, setting down the plates. "This is my real specialty," he says, handing me a fork.

I'm so full, I definitely have a food baby, but

I can't resist trying Nic's dessert. Especially after how good the main course was.

"Oh my God," I say loudly after my first taste. "What is that?"

"Limoncello tiramisu." He laughs as I dive in for another bite.

"You sure know the way to a girl's heart—and to her hips." I grin.

"I'm just happy I'm finally dating a girl who actually eats," he says, then takes a bite himself. "There's nothing worse than cooking for someone who doesn't enjoy food."

"Well, you'll never have that problem with me," I say with a snort. "I think I'm going to become obese if we keep hanging out."

"You'd look beautiful no matter what," he says, smiling at me.

I glance up at him quickly, my heartbeat speeding up. How does he always know the perfect thing to say?

He looks so good, and he's sitting so close to me on the couch that I'm having a hard time resisting reaching over and pulling him on top of me. I watch him carry our empty dessert plates back into the kitchen, admiring the muscles in his broad shoulders.

He walks back and sits even closer to me on the couch, bringing me a fresh glass of sparkling water.

I hope this is the moment we can finally finish what we started a week ago. And if he's even half as good in the bedroom as he is in the kitchen, I'm pretty sure I'm in for a wild night.

"I feel like you're too good to be true," I say, sipping my drink.

"Trust me, I'm far from perfect." He smiles, looking down. "It's me who's lucky to be with you."

"Well, if you're expecting elaborate homemade dinners from me, you might be disappointed. I love to cook, but I've never made anything like that before."

"I don't know," he says. "If I've learned anything about you, it's that you're way too humble, and you always bring the unexpected."

"It's funny, that's exactly how I feel about you," I say quietly, looking into his warm brown eyes.

He leans forward on the couch, and I scoot in

closer to him so our legs are touching. Before I know it, our breaths are mingling and his hand is resting against the back of my neck.

"Gonna kiss you now," he murmurs, his lips almost touching mine.

I make a wordless sound of agreement, and then his mouth meets mine in an urgent kiss. We've been building toward this moment all night. All the laughing and smiles and shared glances have turned into something much hotter and needier than either of us are sure what to do with—other than finish what we started.

His tongue slides into my mouth as our kiss grows fiercer. It's packed with heat and emotion, and dear God, this man can kiss.

I sit up and swing my leg over his so I'm straddling him, sliding my hands across his hard chest. My body feels electrified as he runs his hands down my back, pulling me against him roughly. I arch my back and let out a low moan as he kisses my neck, and I feel my nipples harden inside the cups of my lacy bra. I can't remember ever wanting anyone this badly.

As his lips find mine again, I rock my hips against him, finding that he's hard and . . . holy shit, he's hung like a freaking horse.

"Nic . . ." I groan, pressing my hips forward.

"Yeah, sweetheart?" His voice is rough and growly, and *oh my God*, why is that so hot?

I don't even know why I said his name, don't know what it is I'm asking for. "You're so hard," I murmur.

He makes a groan of frustrated need, and my pulse riots in my throat. "I want you," he admits, pressing one more quick kiss to my lips. "So fucking badly. But what I want and what I'll let myself have are two very different things."

My lust-soaked brain struggles to understand his meaning. But Nic continues, touching my cheek gently with his thumb.

"I've made too many mistakes. I need to do this the right way."

I press my lips to his. He's sweet. I think he's saying he wants to go slow, but as far as I'm concerned, this is the fourth time I've been out with him. I'm ready to toss all my rules out the window.

I slip my hands beneath his shirt, running my fingers along his abs, but he pulls back. He stares deep into my eyes, and there's that same conflicted look he had last Saturday night.

Nic swallows and takes a deep breath, then lifts me off his lap. He brushes a strand of hair out of my face and kisses me again, more sweetly this time, before pulling back again. Whatever inner conflict he's fighting has won—for now, it seems.

"Thanks for coming tonight," he says, standing and running his hands through his hair. "I had a great time. Can I walk you down to your car?"

I'm totally floored by the turn of events. I was sure we were headed for the bedroom, and I already have major lady blue balls. I try not to let him see my disappointment as I stand and pick up my purse, then follow him to the door.

"This was really amazing," I say as we step into the elevator. We're alone, and he lives on the nineteenth floor.

By the time we reach floor thirteen, I can't resist. I turn to Nic and grab his shirt in a fist, pulling him to me. He wraps his arms around me as he slides his tongue into my mouth. We step back so I'm leaning against the wall of the elevator, and his hands run down my chest, gently brushing along my breasts.

I moan as his fingers graze my nipples, and am

about ready to start pulling off clothes when the elevator dings. I have just enough time to regain my composure before the doors open to the lobby. There are a few people standing around, and as we walk past the doorman, he smiles at us, and I wonder if he can tell what we've been up to.

Once we reach my car, I turn to Nic, searching his eyes for signs. I don't know why he keeps ending things before they go too far. I'm not sure what's going on with us, because I've basically been throwing myself at him since we met.

Does he only want to be friends? But who kisses their friends like *that*? Maybe he's just a gentleman, and he actually wants to get to know me before we sleep together.

"Thanks for everything," I say as we reach my car. "You sure know how to sweep a girl off her feet."

"Oh, you haven't seen anything yet." He smirks at me, his gaze playful.

I have to bite my tongue before I ask him *when* I'll get to see it.

He gives me another quick kiss good-bye, sending a shot of heat between my legs before he pulls away. I've never gotten so many mixed signals from a guy before, but maybe it's because I've only dated assholes who were trying to get me into bed as quickly as possible.

Despite my confusion, I know one thing for sure. I'm falling hard for Nic, and nothing—not even Christine's disapproval—can bring me down from this high.

Chapter Fourteen

Nic

I pull open the microwave, and the smell of leftover pasta sauce makes my mouth water. There's only one small serving left over from my date with Elle, and I figure I might as well eat it while I'm still in this post-Elle happiness haze. It feels a little like being drunk. Like I'm invincible. Like nothing in the whole fucking world can touch me.

The only thing keeping this feeling from being the best thing ever? My dick. He's not happy with how last night ended.

Okay, maybe he's not the only one.

I'm not sure how much longer I can keep this up. I wanted her so badly last night. Walking her to her car instead of pounding her into a wall left me with a major case of blue balls. The worst part is I could tell that she wanted me too, and that only made the whole situation—and my cock—ten times harder.

She didn't look upset when I didn't take her to my bed, but I could tell she was confused. And the whole "I'm just a gentleman waiting for the right time" excuse will only work for so long. If I'm not careful, she'll start to suspect that something's up. And if she finds out the truth about me, only one thing will happen. I'll lose her.

There's no way I'm ready to let that happen. Not when I've finally found a sweet, cool, normal girl who checks off every box on my list.

I spoon the now warm leftover sauce onto a plate of cooked pasta just as my phone starts buzzing in my pocket. My brow furrows, and I set my plate down to answer it. Who the fuck is calling me on a Sunday afternoon?

My stomach drops when I see the name on the screen. Christine.

Fuck, fuck, fuck.

"Hey, Christine, how are—"

"What the hell are you doing with Elle?" Her

voice is angry, but firm. She's trying to keep it under control. But there's an edge to it that tells me she could lose it at any moment.

"Look, Christine, I—"

"No, Nic, you listen to me. I don't know what you think you're doing with her, but whatever it is, it's not right. You were hired for one thing only—accompanying her to my wedding. Which was two weeks ago."

I clench my jaw, pushing my hand roughly through my hair. "I know. You're right. But I have to be honest with you. I really like her. More than I expected to."

"She would never be with you if she knew what you were. You need to end this. I never would have set you up with her if I'd known you'd do something as fucked up as this."

"Christine—"

But before I can finish, she hangs up, and the call disconnects.

"Fuck."

I throw my phone onto the table and bury my face into my hands. She's right. Christine is fucking right. I'm a horrible person. I can't believe I'm doing this to Elle.

What the fuck is wrong with me? How did I think this was going to end?

That invincible feeling I had earlier? Fucking gone. I can't believe I was stupid enough to think that I was the right guy for Elle.

My phone chimes again, and I let out a low groan. I don't think I can take any more from Christine. She's made her fucking point. I'm a shitty person who's ruining her best friend's life. Crystal fucking clear.

But it's not Christine. It's Elle.

Had such a good time with you last night. How's your Sunday going?

I groan again. How the fuck am I supposed to respond after just getting chewed out for messing with her head? I can't.

For a moment, I weigh my options. Then I realize if I were to tell her how this all started—that her best friend hired me to pretend to adore her—she would never believe that anything between us was real. Even though these are the most real feelings

I've had in years.

But my feelings don't matter anymore. I have to set them aside and disappear from Elle's life. That's the only way to end this without doing any more damage.

Instead of responding to Elle, I pull up Case's number.

```
Hey, I need the week off to sort
through some personal things.
```

I've barely hit SEND when Case immediately calls me, his anger practically burning a hole in my ear through the phone.

"What the fuck is going on with you? What do you mean you need a full fucking *week* off?"

"Look, Case, I just can't do this right now. I need some time to clear my head. All I'll be able to do in my current state is freak our clients out."

"No, Nic, you need to man the fuck up. I can't keep giving you time off with no notice. How am I supposed to explain to the other guys why they should keep covering your shifts? This is so unprofessional, dude. It's not like you."

"In my professional opinion, I'm not fit to see

any clients this week."

"Why the fuck not?" he roars.

I pull the phone away from my face, rage balling my hand into a fist. The last thing I want to do is open up to Case right now. I don't need to tell him what's going on. It's my fucking life, and he needs to back the hell off.

I take a deep breath before responding. "I just can't, okay?"

Case snorts in frustration, muttering a string of curse words under his breath. "You're unbelievable, Nic. Fucking unbelievable." He hangs up, and the line goes dead.

Nothing like being hung up on twice in a ten-minute time frame.

I can't reply to Elle, so I do the only thing I can—I delete her text and turn my phone to silent.

No longer hungry, I dump my now cold food into the trash.

Instead of sitting on the couch and stewing in my frustration, I decide to go for a run through the park near my house to clear my head.

By the time I get back home, things are slightly more lucid. I don't know what the fuck I'm going to do about Christine, or Elle, or my job, but there is one thing I decided during my run.

I can't let Esther down. It's Sunday, and the thought of her waiting alone at the country club entrance makes my stomach knot up.

I shoot off a text to Case to let him know I'll be there tonight, to which he replies with the thumbs-up emoji.

After throwing on a clean pair of khakis and a crisp button-down, I drive to the country club, where Esther is as kind and pleasant as ever. I do my best to pay attention to her, giving the usual answers about my fake job and friends, but I'm distracted. Elle keeps texting me, and I keep ignoring her.

She was patient and understanding at first, but it's not like me to treat her this way. It doesn't take long for her to realize that something's up.

> Is everything okay? Was it something I said or did?

At least let me know you didn't
die in your sleep.

Seriously, Nic? After everything
that's happened, you're just not
going to respond to me?

It's killing me to leave her hanging like this. But I don't know what else I can do.

When I leave the country club, I drive straight home. I'm not normally the kind of guy to just roll over and give up. But after how this day has gone? I'm ready to spend some quality time on my couch with a bottle of something strong to drown out these fucked-up thoughts running through my head.

And once I get home, that's exactly what I do. After flipping the TV to whatever sports reruns look halfway decent, I change out of my work clothes, grab a couple of cold beers, and stare at the flat screen until my eyes go blurry.

Around ten thirty, a banging on my door shakes me from my trance. My stomach tightens. For a moment, I wonder if it's Elle. And I know if I see her right now, there's no telling what I'll do.

"It's Case, man. Open up."

Fuck.

"Not a good time, Case. I don't want to talk."

"Nic, open this door, or I swear to God, I'll fire you first thing tomorrow."

I open the door to find Case standing there, a scowl on his face and a six-pack in hand.

"Jesus, Nic, you look like shit. Did you see Esther looking like that?"

"Good to see you too."

Case brushes past me and puts the six-pack on my kitchen counter, then cracks open a bottle for each of us. He takes a swig before forcefully setting his bottle back down on the granite, gesturing for me to sit and looking me dead in the eye, his face stone-cold serious.

"We need to talk."

I shrug. "I said what I needed to on the phone. I just need a little time off to clear my head and refocus." Not to mention, I'm pretty sure the only woman I'd be able to get my dick up for is Elle. So, honestly, what fucking good am I right now to his clients?

Case sets down his beer and continues staring at me. "Listen, pretty boy. When I hired you, I knew women would line up to drop their panties for a chance to hop into bed with you. But I also knew you weren't really cut out for this life. You're the kind of guy who eventually meets the right girl and wants to settle down. Is that what's going on right now? With Elle?"

Fuck. I sigh and push my hands through my hair. How does he know all this?

"I don't know. Maybe. But she doesn't know what I am, what I do for a living. She'd never be with me if she knew the truth."

"You don't know that until you talk to her about it. Don't underestimate her. If she's as awesome as you say she is, I bet she'll get it."

"I kind of doubt that."

We pause, quickly downing our beers. Case changes the subject as we keep drinking, and by beer three, we're laughing and talking about the early days, when he first hired me. I had no idea what I was doing or what the job actually was. Becoming a professional escort had a steep learning curve, but it was one hell of a ride.

"Remember when that cougar tried to tie you

up without discussing it as part of your contract first? You were such a naive little pup. So many things to learn." Case laughs, shaking his head.

"I was into it, man! That was all good."

He chuckles, shaking his head.

"Let's just not talk about that first time I was with Gia," I say, smirking.

Case laughs out loud. "I still have that fucking email. It's hilarious."

I roll my eyes. "Ha-ha, motherfucker."

"Yeah, well, you learned quick. One of our best guys, really."

He claps a hand on my shoulder, and we smile at each other. My head is starting to swim a little from the beers, but it's clear enough for worry and doubt to creep in.

"I don't know what else I could do for work. This job is all I've ever known."

"Eh, you'll figure it out. You're a smart guy. Plus, who could say no to that pretty face of yours?"

"If I can't actually do the work? Lots of people."

Case laughs, remembering another job I botched back in my early days. I laugh along with him while he recounts the story, but in the back of my mind, all I can think about is Elle.

I was serious when I said there's nothing else I can do besides this job. My résumé won't be winning anyone over, that's for sure. And I've only known Elle for a few weeks now.

How can I change my entire life for a shot with a girl—no matter how amazing or perfect she seems for me—when I have no idea if we'll even work out once she learns the truth about me?

Chapter Fifteen

Elle

All day, my stomach has been in knots. I couldn't even enjoy my lunch at one of my favorite sushi spots downtown.

After my amazing date with Nic last weekend, he stopped responding to my texts or calls. At first, I was hurt, then mad, but now I'm just worried. It's not like him, and the only logical explanation is that he's sick or hurt, or . . . worse. I've been counting down the minutes until it's five o'clock and I can go to his place and check on him.

I glance at the clock again, and relief floods through me when I see it's finally time to go. Rising to my feet, I grab my purse from the file cabinet drawer where I store it during the day, and shove my phone inside.

"Hey, Elle!" Lindsey from reception stops beside my desk, smiling at me.

"Hi, Lindsey. What's going on?"

Even if I'm not exactly in the mood to chitchat, Lindsey is sweet. We go to coffee together sometimes, so I can't blow her off and rush for the parking lot like I want to.

"Me and Samantha from accounting are going to grab a drink. The new place around the corner has great happy-hour specials."

I smile politely and place the strap of my purse over my shoulder. "Sorry, I can't tonight."

"Plans?" She grins.

My stomach churns uneasily. I haven't told anyone about Nic yet, not after Christine's reaction, but maybe it's time I do. It wouldn't hurt to get a little friendly female advice.

I chew on my lip and meet her gaze. "Actually, I'm not sure. There's this guy I've been seeing, and I haven't been able to get in touch with him the last couple of days. We had this amazing date, and then . . . poof, nothing. I'm wondering if he's sick or something."

She makes a face at me.

"What?" I ask.

Lindsay presses her lips into a line. "It sounds like you're getting blown off. That sucks." Then she grins again and flips her hair over one shoulder. "Which means you should definitely come out to happy hour. I'll buy you a margarita."

I shake my head. "Nic wouldn't do that. He must be sick or dead. That's the only explanation."

Lindsay's eyebrows dart up. "Trust me, guys do skeevy shit like this all the time."

I huff out a sigh. "Either way, I'm going to go over to his place and check on him."

I know him well enough to know that it's not like him to blow a woman off like that, even if he isn't interested. At least, I thought I did.

A guarded expression flashes across her features before she smiles at me again. "If you say so. Good luck."

"Thanks."

We start off together toward the glass doors in the lobby, but each step makes my stomach churn with nerves. What if she's right? What if I totally read our date wrong? But my curiosity has gotten the better of me, and I need to know what's going on.

When I reach Nic's place and see his black Tesla parked out front, my mood changes from worried to pissed off.

I take the elevator to his floor and knock on his door. Then I take a step back, placing my hands on my hips in anticipation of what's about to happen. I'm so mad now I'm practically shaking. But I'm here to get answers. And if he acts like a total asshole, I am so out of here.

After a few moments, I hear footsteps from inside, and Nic opens the door. We stare at each other for a moment, and I can tell immediately that something's wrong. I'm fully ready to ask him what the hell is going on when I pause to take in his disheveled hair and his deep brown eyes, which are more heavily lidded than usual.

"Elle," he says, his voice cracking. He places one tanned hand against the door frame as he takes me in. "What are you doing here?" he asks, slurring his words slightly.

"Are you drunk?" I ask, incredulous. I don't know what I was expecting when I came here, but it wasn't to see calm, cool, and collected Nic drunk like he's just attended his first frat party.

He shakes his head as he leans against the door frame. Despite how mad I am, I can't help but notice how good he looks in his casual T-shirt and jeans. It isn't fair. How does he still look this sexy, even when he's totally obliterated?

"I had a few drinks with a friend last night." He shrugs.

He looks at me again, not quite meeting my eyes, and I can see that he's anxious about something. I can also tell that he had more than just a few drinks, but I decide not to push it.

"You caught me at a really bad time. You should go."

"What's going on with you?" I demand, ignoring him. "I was worried sick about you."

"Elle, can we please not do this right now?" He rubs his face in his hands, letting out a little sigh.

"Yes, we're going to do this now. You invite me over, cook for me, and then you totally ghosted me." I push my way past him into the apartment. He doesn't try to stop me, probably because he can barely stand up straight. "Who does that?"

"Please, can we talk about anything but that?" he pleads, watching me as I set my purse down and turn back to face him.

I notice the empty beer cans strewn across the coffee table, along with a half-empty bottle of whiskey. Then I take him in again. He's still leaning against the door, and he looks miserable.

My anger fades as I look into his eyes. I can tell that whatever's going on, he really is torn up about it. And if it is actually something serious, I don't want to come in here and be a total bitch just because he didn't text me for a few days.

"When's the last time you ate?" I ask, my voice softening.

He shrugs. "Earlier today, I guess."

"Come," I say as I walk into his kitchen and pull open the cupboards, checking out what he has.

He follows me, standing uncertainly in the kitchen doorway. I fill a glass of water and set it down on the table, then I grab his hand and lead him to a chair.

"Sit. And drink this." I'm still annoyed that he blew me off, but I'm willing to believe he has a decent reason for it.

As he drinks his water, I pull ingredients out of the fridge and put together a quick stir fry, figuring the rice will soak up some of the alcohol. I glance at him as I cook, making sure he's drinking the water. After a lifetime of always being the designated driver, I've had plenty of practice playing nurse for highly intoxicated people. And although the only place I really want to play nurse with Nic is in the bedroom, it's my instinct to help him right now.

Fifteen minutes later, I set two steaming plates on the table, where he's holding his head in his hands. I fish out two Advil from my purse and set them next to the plate of food.

"Take these," I say, refilling his water.

He lifts his head from his hands as I bring him a fresh glass of water. He seems embarrassed, and it's understandable. After all, I was in his position a couple of weeks ago, and I know it's not a great feeling to be obnoxiously drunk in front of the person you were hoping to sleep with.

"Here, eat this. It will help," I say gently, pushing his plate toward him.

"Why are you being so nice?" he asks quietly after he swallows the pills.

"I don't know," I tell him honestly, and then pause for a moment. "I guess you just seem like you need some kindness right now."

There's something about him that I can't be mad at. I came here ready to demand answers, but I guess my motherly instincts took over. Or maybe it's that every time I look into those brown eyes, I can't think about anything except for how gorgeous he is. I'm only human, after all.

Nic nods, giving me a weak smile. I can already tell he's becoming more like himself again as he holds my gaze. I look away and gesture at him to start eating. He eats quickly, without speaking, finishing his food in just a few minutes.

Since it's dinnertime, I eat alongside him quietly, even though I'm completely curious about what happened to make him go off the deep end like this.

"Maybe I'm just drunk, but this is really good," he says, glancing at me as he takes his last bite.

"It should be good hangover food." I smile, shrugging. "So hopefully you won't feel like you've been hit by a Mack truck when you wake up tomorrow."

"Sorry about earlier," he says, taking our plates over to the sink. "I'm usually not this much of a mess. It's really sweet of you to cook for me." He pauses. "Especially after the way I've been acting."

I watch him, not sure what to say. The fact that

he's acknowledging how strange he's been acting makes me want to ask even more questions. I figured he'd just deny everything and try to make me feel crazy, which is what my ex used to do. I want to ask a million questions, but Nic seems like he's really struggling with something, and I want him to tell me when he's ready.

He sits up quickly, like he just remembered something. "I got you a present." He leaves the kitchen, and when he comes back, he's holding a large bag that he sets down on the table.

Shocked, I pull it toward me, wondering what he could possibly have gotten me. As I peek inside, I realize he bought review books for the bar exam.

I stare at him, wide-eyed and open-mouthed, unable to speak. I'm so touched that he cares that much, I forget all the anger I've been harboring over the last couple of days.

"You didn't have to do this."

He shakes his head. "I wanted to. I also signed you up for a review class. It starts next week." Smiling, he says, "I know I should have probably checked with you first. I know you're going to ace the bar, and I thought this would help."

When I still don't say anything, too overwhelmed to speak, he seems nervous.

"Did I cross a line?" he asks uncertainly.

My throat tightens with emotion and I shake my head, finally recovering from my shock. "Not at all. Nic, this is the nicest thing anyone's ever done for me."

A smile spreads across my face as I look from the books back to him. To have someone believe in me like this, especially someone I've known such a short time, means a lot to me. Plus, those review classes are really expensive. I've looked into them before, and I'm in awe at his generosity.

He smiles at me, that sweet sort of crooked smile, and my entire world shifts. All the anger and worry I felt slide away.

"Are you okay?" I ask.

He reaches out and takes my hand, giving it a gentle squeeze. "I will be."

"You feel all right? Still drunk?"

He smirks at me. "I wasn't drunk, I was . . . okay, I was drunk. But I actually feel pretty damn good now." He laces his fingers with mine and tugs me toward the couch.

"Will you tell me what happened?"

Nic looks down at his hands, and he's quiet for a second. "I want to. I will when the time is right."

I trust him. I'm not sure what happened to make him clam up, but I believe him when he says he'll explain it all.

The air between us grows heavier, and I become aware of the fact that we're sitting just inches apart.

Still holding my hand, Nic slides his thumb along my inner wrist, and just that simple touch sends pleasure skittering along my nerve endings. He leans closer, and my heartbeat starts to riot.

"I don't deserve this," he whispers before his lips press to mine.

I kiss him back, and oh dear God, I've missed this. My lips part in silent invitation, and Nic slides his tongue softly against mine.

I forgot how sexy and sensual he is, almost even without trying. His kisses are slow and deep and perfect. He tastes like whiskey and heaven, and as his hands slip into my hair, I make a tiny noise of approval.

He reaches down and lifts me onto his lap in

one quick motion as we continue to kiss. I wrap my legs around his hips and put my arms around his neck, pressing my body against his hard chest. I love the feel of his firm stomach and chest, and can't help running my hands along the muscles beneath his T-shirt.

"Elle . . ." He groans when I touch his stomach, just above his belt.

I can feel him hard and ready between my thighs, and my breath catches in my throat.

His gaze drops from mine, traveling slowly down my body, making me shiver with desire as it comes to rest on my breasts. They feel heavy against my black bra, and my nipples are hard underneath the thin fabric. He slides his hands down my shoulders, gently cupping my breasts before running a thumb across each of my nipples. I moan, arching my back, wanting more.

"Should we take this to your bedroom?" I ask, my voice breathy.

He pauses, meeting my gaze. His eyes are dark and heavy with desire, but his hesitation makes me nervous. I've never wanted someone more in my life, and I don't think I'll be able to stand it if he stops this now.

Chapter Sixteen

Nic

How the fuck am I supposed to say no to her again?

For weeks now, I've resisted her. Told myself that nothing good could come from acting on the desires she stirs in me. I fought with myself, pushed those desires away. Tried my best to ignore them, blue balls be damned.

But now she's here and sexier than ever. The way she barged in here to check on me, cooked for me, made me eat? It's like I traded one buzz for another.

I've never been with anyone as sweet and caring as Elle. I have friends, sure, but no one who cares about me this way. Case only cares if I'm out making him money or not. And Elle isn't just anyone. I care about her too. And fuck, she looks so goddamn tempting.

Even I have my limits.

Sweeping her into my arms, I carry her to my bedroom. She squeals as I lift her, her breasts swaying with the motion. She smiles and throws her arms around me, nuzzling her face into my neck, teasing my skin with her tongue. My cock swells as I imagine all the other things her tongue can do.

I lay her down on my bed, admiring the way her supple body looks in my space. She arches her back, reaching for me, hungry for my touch. Just the sight of her wanting me so much is almost too much to handle.

Almost.

Lowering my body over her, I bring my lips to hers. Our mouths crash together, our tongues exploring as my hands wander her body. I run my thumb over her stiffening nipple, causing a small whimper to escape from her. She bucks her hips into me, grinding against my erection, and the sensation drives me crazy.

More. All I want is more. To push every inch into her, to thrust myself inside her. Make her feel as full and complete as she makes me feel.

God, we've waited so long for this.

I take my time stripping Elle of her dress pants and button-up shirt. Next, I slide her lacy panties down her hips and reach behind her to unclasp her bra. Heat rises to her cheeks as she meets my eyes.

Elle looks good with clothes on, but she's a whole other kind of sexy when she's naked. Her long coppery hair tumbling over her shoulders, her full, round breasts just begging to be kissed. She's the most gorgeous thing I've ever seen.

Moving over top of her, I bring my lips to her neck, sucking a little on the tender skin there as my hand cups one gorgeous tit. Elle makes a small whimpered sound of approval. Then I move down her chest, kissing and licking every inch of her perfect breasts. She wriggles under the touch of my tongue, each movement bringing her hips closer to mine, the warmth between her legs teasing me.

When I reach her stomach, I trail my tongue over the softness of her skin, and a thought occurs to me. I'm about to do something I haven't done since I got into the escort business.

Suddenly, I know exactly what I want to do to Elle, exactly how I want to show her how much she means to me. This whole time I thought oral wasn't something I enjoyed doing, but now I know that I've never had the right woman underneath me to make me want to go down on her. Elle is obviously my muse. I smile at the thought.

I move down to kiss her inner thigh, placing my hands on either side of her hips, sucking and biting on the delicate skin. When I move lower, Elle props herself on her elbows, reaching to run her fingers through my hair as she gazes down at me.

"Nic, you don't have to," she whispers as I turn to kiss her other leg, getting closer and closer to her hot center.

It's the only rule left I haven't broken. No oral sex.

It's not that I've never done it before, it's just that there's something so intimate about it—kissing someone in their most vulnerable place—that I always wanted to save it for the woman I choose to spend my life with. To keep it as a small gift, the only penance I can offer after the way I've made a living for all these years.

And in this moment, there's nothing I want to do more. Even if this all falls apart, if Elle isn't that woman for me, at least I will have done this for her.

At least I will have shown her how important she truly is to me.

"I want to." I sit up and strip off my T-shirt, then unbutton my jeans to make more room for the erection that barely fits in my pants before I lean back down over her.

With my eyes still on hers, I place my mouth over her core, licking and kissing her softly to give her time to adjust to the sensation and let the pleasure build. Soon, she's moaning as my tongue slides over her center, circling her hard little pearl.

"You taste so good," I murmur, and she can only purr in response, her body writhing to the rhythm of my tongue.

I slide one hand up her body, rolling her fully erect nipple between my thumb and forefinger. The other hand I wrap around her thigh, anchoring myself to her center. Her hips roll and buck against my mouth as she gets closer and closer. Her whimpers and moans grow more insistent, and her whole body moves with pleasure. Suddenly, her back arches violently as her orgasm crashes through her, wave after wave washing over her.

As her heavy breathing subsides, she pulls me closer, and I balance my weight over her, my thick erection wedged between our bodies.

I want her to touch me so badly. I haven't been touched simply for pleasure in so long—by someone who wants me for me—and the emotion of the moment is hitting me much harder than I thought it would.

Her lips hover just inches from mine. When she finally speaks, her voice is breathy. "That was . . ."

"You're amazing," I tell her, drawing her face to mine for a slow, deep kiss.

With a smile, she reaches down and pushes my jeans and boxers down to take my cock in her hand, slowly stroking my thick length. Her fist squeezes the base before drawing up and over me. A low groan escapes from the back of my throat.

She slides her thumb over my tip, spreading a single drop of wetness over the head. Then she runs her hand achingly slowly down my shaft again, and as it comes back up, I let out a low hiss between my teeth. She is so perfect, so sexy, and part of me still can't believe she's touching me.

"Stroke me, baby," I groan out.

Elle's eyes grow wide as she fully takes in my size for the first time. Then her fists close around me—both hands—and her pace quickens. I rock my hips forward, thrusting into her hands, and let out a grunt.

My fingers tangle in her hair and my lips find hers as her hand moves over my aching dick. My balls tighten, and I'm somehow already close.

"God, Nic," she murmurs, one small palm pressing against my abs. "I need you."

I reach over to the bedside table and pull a condom from the top drawer. I get tested regularly, and I'm sure Elle is clean too, but the fact that she doesn't know about my past or what I do for a living . . . it makes me feel like I shouldn't expose her to anything she doesn't know about. Quickly unwrapping it, I roll it over my length.

Warning bells ring in my head. Part of me knows I should stop this, but the other part, the primal part of me who wants to fuck her into next week, knows that's no longer possible.

Sliding her down on the bed, I align my hips with hers and place a pillow under her hips. Elle watches me with wide, curious eyes, and a pretty flush colors her cheeks.

"You sure you want this?" I ask, touching her hip with my fingertips as my other hand squeezes the base of my cock to calm myself the fuck down.

"So much. Now, come here."

She opens her arms to me, beckoning me forward, and I obey, aligning myself with her warm, wet center as our chests touch.

I push myself inside her, just the tip, watching her face for any trace of pain. "Is this okay?"

She opens her eyes to look at me, her brows scrunched together, out of pain or pleasure, I can't tell. She nods, brushing a few stray hairs from her forehead with her fingers. "Don't stop."

I slowly enter her again, savoring every warm, velvety inch of her. Elle moans, and I let out a long breath when my hips meet hers. Totally filling her.

Fuck.

Nothing has ever felt this good.

With one hand on the bed to support myself, I place the other under her neck, pulling her face to mine. We kiss as I move over her in deep, even strokes, the pressure building in me with each thrust.

I watch as Elle's expression changes, lust filling her features. Every single thing she's feeling is written all over her face, and I love seeing it happen.

I can feel myself getting close, but I don't want this to end, so I briefly withdraw and roll onto my back, pulling Elle on top of me. Within moments, I enter her again, my cock growing somehow stiffer at the way her breasts bounce.

Placing my hands on her hips, I guide her movements, pulling her down hard each time I thrust up. I maneuver my hand so I can rub her clit with my thumb, and the sensation drives her crazy.

She throws her head back, her hair cascading over her shoulders, and her perfect hourglass figure is the best sight I've ever seen. Her breathing becomes ragged, her chest heaving, and I can tell she's getting close by the way her body tightens around me.

Pressure builds behind my cock again, but this time, instead of backing off, I thrust harder, pumping into her faster than before. I need to make her come for me again.

Suddenly, she's clenching around me, crying out as she comes, and it's just enough to make me follow her over the edge. Elle clutches my biceps, her eyes falling closed as her climax washes through her. Finally, her body relaxes and she collapses on top of me, the feel of her skin on mine even better than before.

We stay that way for a few moments, our bodies entwined, our chests rising and falling together. I've never felt closer to another person, never felt more connected, more in tune. If any part of me tried to deny it before, there's no denying it now.

I'm in trouble. Great, big, fucking, wonderful trouble.

Chapter Seventeen

Elle

We're lying side by side in his bed, and there's no place on earth I'd rather be.

"Wow," Nic says, propping himself up on an elbow. "That was . . ."

"Worth the wait?" I ask, looking up at him with a grin.

His eyes meet mine, and he caresses my cheek with his thumb. "Definitely worth the wait."

He leans down and kisses me gently on the forehead before rolling over.

"Do you need any water?" he asks, standing and stretching.

Biting my lip, I admire the muscles in his back as they flex. Every time I look at him, it's like he gets even sexier.

"That'd be great, actually, thanks," I say, leaning back against the pillows.

"I figured after all that moaning, your throat might be a little dry." He smirks, pulling on a pair of shorts.

I snort and throw one of his pillows at him. He laughs as he leaves the room, and I slide back down underneath the covers, still not ready to leave my post-sex haze.

When Nic doesn't come back right away, I get curious. I slip into an oversized T-shirt I find in his closet and head into the living room, wondering what could have distracted him. I notice that the bathroom light is on, and I see Nic bending over the tub.

"Wait, don't look yet," he says quickly when he sees me coming in, but it's too late. Nic has set up a bath, complete with candles and rose-scented bubble bath.

I can't believe it. This is more than anyone's ever done for me. "What's all this?"

"It's for you," he says, putting his hands on my shoulders.

I pause for a moment as he lights the final candle, still more than a little stunned at how thoughtful he is. "Did you grow up in a romance novel or something?"

"I'm not usually a romantic guy," he says, smirking at me. "But for the right girl . . ."

"I am pretty lucky, aren't I?" I put my arms around his neck, and he gives me a short, sweet kiss. I tighten my hold, wanting him closer, but he pulls back.

"You're not coming in?" I ask, disappointed.

"This is just for you to relax, to say thank you for being so sweet to me earlier," he says. "But don't worry, I'll still be here when you're done. And I'll be picturing you in here, naked." He winks at me as he pulls the door shut.

I smile to myself as I pull off the T-shirt and slip into the tub, breathing in the rose scent. There's even a glass of ice water sitting on the counter for me, along with a fluffy white towel.

I can't believe how thoughtful he is. He's nothing like the playboy Christine tried to make him out to be. I shake my head, not wanting those thoughts to even enter my brain right now. In this moment, I just want to be happy with Nic.

After a while, I decide I've had enough alone time. The warm tub, romantic candles, and calming scent of the bath are making me tingle between my legs, and I want to see Nic again. I towel off and wander into the living room. I find him sitting on the couch, fully clothed again, sipping a water. When he looks up at me, his mouth drops open.

"I got lonely," I say, watching him take me in. His eyes move from my face, along my curves barely concealed by the towel, down to my legs and back up.

I saunter over to him and kneel in front of him on the floor. He swallows, watching as I unzip his jeans.

"What are you doing?" he asks hoarsely, parting his legs so I can kneel between them.

"Returning the favor from earlier," I say, pulling down his jeans and boxer briefs to reveal all eight perfect inches of him. Dear God, this man . . .

He's already hard when I take him in my mouth, and I run my tongue along the tip of his erection. He groans as I move my lips farther and farther down his length, gently caressing his balls as I move my head up and down. He grips my hair in his hands as I move faster, and the sound of his heavy breathing is turning me on more than I expected.

"Fuck, Elle." He groans, his hand tensing on the back of my neck. "I'm going to come soon," he says, his breathing ragged as his hands slide down to my shoulders.

I take my mouth off of him and straddle him on the couch. He unknots the towel fastened around me and tosses it onto the floor.

I kiss him, my tongue slipping into his mouth as his hands caress my breasts, teasing my nipples before sliding down my sides and then along my legs. He runs his hand along my inner thigh before touching me gently between my legs. I shudder as his fingers begin to work. He is so talented. So good. At everything.

"You're so wet, baby," he groans.

It feels so good that I can't wait any longer. I pull his hand away and rub myself along his erection, slowly and then faster. We're both breathing heavily, and when I finally guide him inside me, I let out a moan as his erection fills me. He moves a hand to my breast, pinching my nipple as I rock my hips faster and faster against him.

"You feel so good," he whispers, moving his hand to my other breast.

I'm rocking harder and harder against him, wanting him fully inside me. He kisses my neck, and I arch my back as he thrusts and grips my backside to pull my hips closer, lifting me up and down over him. I let out a cry as he plunges even deeper inside me, and feel pressure building in my core.

"Don't stop." I moan as he thrusts harder, and my head falls back.

Nic bends to kiss my breasts, murmuring sweet little encouragements about how sexy I am riding him. I can't catch my breath as our bodies rock against each other, and when I come, I lose control, my entire body shuddering with waves of pleasure.

Nic slows his pace, watching me with a hooded gaze. "Fuck. So sexy," he groans. "Gonna come soon." Still gripping my ass in both hands, Nic thrusts up, his eyes sinking closed as if this is the best pleasure he's ever felt. "Where do you want it?"

"Inside me," I murmur, bringing my lips to his.

He groans again, hugging me close as he finally climaxes.

We don't move for a few minutes afterward, waiting for our breathing to slow. Nic brushes a strand of hair out of my face, looking into my eyes.

His look even sexier than ever, hazy from sex and full of emotion. Slowly, I climb off of him and pull on my towel, knotting it at my breasts again.

He stands up and presses a tender kiss to my lips, then pulls on his briefs and T-shirt. We walk together into his bedroom, and I start to get dressed.

Since he hasn't asked me to stay, I don't want to wear out my welcome. Things tonight have been perfect, but I can't forget about how he disappeared on me a couple of days. The last thing I want to do is rush anything if he's feeling overwhelmed.

"I should get going. I have to get up early tomorrow."

I feel his gaze on me as I pull my clothes on, but he doesn't say anything. It seems like he's deep in thought, but I decide not to ask about it. There will be time to get answers later. For now, I just want to savor everything that's happened over the past few hours.

"I'll call you tomorrow," he says as he walks me to the door. He holds the sides of my face and gives me a gentle kiss on the forehead before I leave.

Despite all my unanswered questions, I'm floating as I walk to my car. I know it's crazy, but this man makes me feel like I can do anything.

I only hope that he's being truthful with me when he says he'll call me tomorrow. I'm not sure I can handle him ghosting me again after the night we've just shared.

"Girl, did you get a facial or something? You're glowing." Christine looks me up and down.

I met her at the farmers' market this morning to do some shopping since we haven't seen each other in over a week. I'm not surprised she commented; I've been in a particularly good mood ever since my night with Nic earlier this week. I haven't exactly been in a rush to tell her about the developments with Nic, but it seems dishonest to keep it a secret now that we've had sex.

"Well, to be honest," I say, picking up a bouquet of flowers and smelling them. "It's Nic. He's amazing, Christine. I can't believe you set me up with him."

I try not to gush, but I can't stop myself. All I want to do is scream from the rooftops that I met the most amazing, thoughtful man in the world. Not to mention he's about as sinfully sexy as it gets.

"Elle, you're not still seeing him, are you?" Christine asks, her face crumpling.

"Yeah, I am. What's wrong with that?" I ask, purposely playing dumb. If she wants to finally tell me what's so bad about Nic, she needs to just come out with it. "You're the one who set us up. I'm sick of you acting like it's so wrong that we're hanging out."

Christine pauses with an apple in her hand. She looks at the ground for a few seconds before looking back up at me, biting her lip.

"Christine? What's wrong?"

She seems conflicted, but it's time she told me the truth about Nic. I'm tired of her cryptic warnings about him, and I'm going to push her until she finally admits what her problem is.

"Look, don't get mad," she says, setting the apple down and turning to face me. "But you were really stressed out about seeing Jeremy at the wedding, and I knew he was going to be there with that new bimbo, and I felt really bad about it. I just wanted you to have fun."

"What are you talking about? Isn't that why

you set me up with Nic?"

"The thing is, it wasn't really a setup. Or it was, but not like that." She looks into my eyes, anxiety etched on her face. "I don't really know Nic from college."

What? My heart is pounding hard. I don't know what she's talking about, but it suddenly feels like someone dropped a lead weight into my stomach.

"Christine, what do you mean?"

Even though I've asked the question, some part of me doesn't want to know. The past few weeks have been so amazing, and I have a horrible feeling she's about to drop a huge bomb on me.

Before continuing, she takes a deep breath. "I hired him. I just wanted you to have a date for the weekend to pick your spirits up, and that would be it. I didn't think he'd keep pursuing you after." She waves her hands in the air. "I didn't think it would lead to all this."

I feel like I've been sucker punched, and my heart just skipped about fifteen beats.

"Christine, what are you talking about? You hired him from where?"

"He's a male escort, Elle. He sleeps with women for money. But I didn't hire him for that; it was just to hang out with you and make sure you had fun at the wedding. I specifically told him to be a gentleman, and I definitely didn't tell him it was okay to pursue you after the wedding was over."

Christine won't look at me, and I suddenly feel faint. I try to breathe deeply, but I can't seem to catch my breath.

"But he said he worked in finance . . ." My words trail off as all the pieces come together.

The reason Christine has been so weird, and why Nic will never talk about his work. The way he kept hesitating to sleep with me, and all those little moments where he seemed guarded and I had no idea why.

Now I know why he blew me off those few days; he was probably afraid of us getting closer, given that our entire relationship so far has been based on a lie. All the clues have been there and I've missed them all, consumed by my feelings for him.

But he was paid to make me feel these things, and he's damn good at his job. I'll give him that.

Nic is a fraud.

I feel disgusted with myself. I had sex with him—without a condom.

Oh God. I feel sick.

I stare at Christine, tears filling my eyes, but I don't say anything else. After weeks of questioning, I finally have all the answers I need.

Chapter Eighteen

Nic

The knot that's been forming in my stomach all day tightens even more as I walk through the door to Case's house. Pausing in the foyer, I take a good look around, appreciating the little details I've taken for granted all these years. The pristine marble, the framed artwork, the sleek and sturdy furniture set over long, patterned rugs.

Case runs a tight ship, both in his business and in his home. The two have become one and the same, really. He's always treated each of us escorts like family. Which makes what I'm about to do ten thousand times harder.

I walk through the living room, nodding to a couple of the guys lounging and watching TV on the couch.

"Hey, Nic, long time no see. How's it going?" Ryder smiles and leans forward, resting his forearms on his knees.

I notice the half-finished beer on the side table next to him but don't say anything. I'm in no position to judge. "Doing well. It's good to see you. Is Case in his office?"

Ryder leans back, a smirk on his lips. "Yeah, he's around. Heard you've had a lot going on lately."

I clench my teeth, annoyed that the guys have been talking about me. Not that I should be surprised. They're not judging or anything. Just concerned.

"That's what I'm hoping to talk to him about, actually."

Ryder nods, turning his attention back to the TV. "Well, I'll let you get to it. See you around."

I nod and turn to make my way down the hall to Case's office. When I reach the open door, I knock and poke my head in. "This a bad time?"

Case looks up and shakes his head. He's dressed in jeans and a T-shirt, and by the looks of it, he hasn't shaved in a few days. Normally, he's so well put together, it makes me wonder what's going on. "Wasn't expecting to see you so soon. Come on in."

I take a seat at the leather chair in front of his desk, crossing my ankle over my knee. The knot in my stomach has somehow grown larger.

Fuck. Why is this so hard?

"So, what's up?" Case asks after finishing typing whatever he was working on.

"You know I appreciate everything you've done for me. That I've enjoyed this job, and value you as a friend, right?"

Case's eyebrows draw together and he nods slowly. "What's going on? Just spit it out, Nic."

"I wanted to let you know that I'm officially resigning. I'm in love with Elle, and leaving this job is the best chance I have to be with her."

He stares at me for a few moments before responding. "Well, I can't say I'm surprised. Always knew you'd settle down and get out of this business one day. Have you told her yet?"

I shake my head, rubbing the back of my neck. "I wanted to make this official first."

Case leans back in his chair, weighing my words. "How do you think she'll take it?"

"No idea. But being with her is the most alive I've felt in years. I'd never forgive myself if I didn't do everything in my power to try."

At this, he smiles and folds his hands, resting them behind his head. "Well, what are you still doing here? Go get your girl."

"You sure you're not pissed?" The last thing I want to do is burn a bridge. Yeah, he was my boss, but I also consider him a friend.

"I'm not pissed. Does it suck to lose you? Fuck yes." His lips curl up into a smirk. "You made me a lot of money."

I chuckle and shake my head. How I'm going to make money going forward isn't something I want to think about right now. One thing at a time. The first thing on my list of priorities is talking to Elle so I can finally tell her the truth.

I leave Case's house feeling ten feet tall. He took my news way better than I thought, and having his support concerning Elle means more than I thought it would.

I drive straight to a flower shop, pick out the

most beautiful bouquet I can find, and head to Elle's place. We haven't talked since that incredible night a few days ago, so I'm not sure what she's up to, but I feel too amazing to go another minute without seeing her.

When I get to Elle's door, I knock and take a step back as nervous energy buzzes through my veins. It's crazy all the things she makes me feel. The old Nic never got nervous or excited to see a woman.

I stand there for a few minutes, flowers in hand, but she doesn't answer. I pull out my phone and try calling. No answer.

I shoot her a text asking where she is, but when she doesn't respond after several minutes, I decide to get back in my car and head home. If she was home, she'd answer. She's probably just out running errands or something. I'll wait until she responds, and then I'll go to wherever she is.

At home, I try to distract myself. I flip through some TV channels, but nothing holds my attention. I try making some food, but by the time it's done, I'm not hungry and don't want to eat it. No matter what I try, I keep obsessively checking my phone. That knot in my stomach from earlier? Yeah, it's back with a fucking vengeance.

Something doesn't feel right.

I don't understand why she's ignoring me. We've had our issues in the past—mainly me acting like an asshole—but I thought we'd made up and had an amazing night.

I spend the rest of the day racking my brain for what might be bothering her. Did I say something that upset her? Was the sex not as good for her as I thought? Is she mad I didn't text her sooner?

But none of that sounds like the Elle I know. If she had a problem with me, she would say something. I think the fact that she showed up on my doorstep when I wouldn't text her back proves that.

Unless something happened that would keep her from doing that.

As I mechanically prepare another meal I don't have the appetite to eat, I can't keep my worries about Elle under control. It's not like her to ignore me at all, especially not for this long. I can't even entertain the idea that something horrible might have happened to her without feeling like I'm going to fucking lose it.

Just as I'm starting to panic, I remember I still have Christine's number. I frantically compose a text to her.

> Hey, Christine. Have you heard
> from Elle? Having a hard time
> getting a hold of her.

Pacing around my kitchen, I wait impatiently for her to reply. But when my phone chimes and I unlock the screen, the words I read make me feel like someone punched me in the stomach.

> Yes, I have. I told her the truth
> about you.

I drop my phone on the counter. It feels like all the air has been sucked out of my lungs. I can't believe Christine did that. I should have let her know that I was planning to tell Elle myself. Maybe then she would have understood, would have given me the chance to explain.

My phone chimes again and I scramble to check it, a small part of me still hopeful that Elle will reply.

But it's just Christine. Rubbing salt into my wounds.

> It's over, Nic. She doesn't want
> anything to do with you. With ei-
> ther of us.

I throw my phone across the room. I can't take this anymore. Sinking into a chair, I bury my face in my hands, crushed under the weight of what all this means.

It should have been me who told her. I was ready to explain why I went into escort work, prove to her it was all in the past. I quit for her, left behind the most successful opportunity I've ever had in exchange for the chance to start a life with her. A new one. The kind of life I've always wanted but was never sure I could have or even deserved. With her by my side, I thought anything was possible.

Now, it's hopeless. The dream I thought I was about to be living is gone. Over. Dead. I was stupid to think she'd ever want someone like me.

I grab a bottle of whiskey from my liquor cabinet and take a few swigs. Just as I settle into my seat on the couch, my phone rings from across the room. I sigh and go to answer it, a small part of me still hoping I'll hear Elle's voice on the other end.

But instead, it's Case's voice, which only makes me feel worse.

"Hey, I'm surprised you even answered. I was hoping you'd be too busy making sweet love to your lady right about now."

When I don't answer, Case clears his throat. "You all right, Nic? How'd it go?"

I sigh, then chug more whiskey. "It didn't."

"You're going to have to give me more than that."

"Christine told her before I could. Now she won't talk to me."

"Fuck, man, I'm sorry. What are you going to do?"

"Looks like I'm halfway through this bottle of whiskey. After that, no clue."

Case pauses, the silence on the phone making me feel even more like shit. "Well, you can always come back to work if you want to."

I snort, shaking my head and running my hand over my face. "I can't go back to that life, Case. What's done is done. Even if I can't be with Elle, the time I had with her showed me that there's more to life than this."

"Whatever makes you happy, dude. Hey, you still have your old-lady client tomorrow. Want me to call her and cancel?"

Rubbing my temple with one hand, I close my

eyes to think about it. Of all my clients, Esther was always the sweetest. And the thought of canceling on her at the last minute makes me feel like an absolutely worthless piece of shit. I couldn't do it before, and I can't do it now.

"No, it's fine. I'll go. Just one last time so I can tell her good-bye."

I arrive at the country club the next day feeling like shit. I make a quick stop in the restroom to splash some water on my face before meeting Esther in the dining room.

When I look in the mirror, I hardly recognize the asshole staring back at me. Bloodshot eyes, gray bags hanging underneath them, messy hair. The only plus side is that it's an accurate depiction of what's happening on the inside.

I find Esther at our usual table, and she rises to greet me. We hug, and I kiss her on the cheek like always, choosing to ignore the worried look on her face.

"You look terrible," she says, leaning toward me after we sit down.

"I feel terrible." I prop my elbows on the table and run my hands through my hair.

"What is it? Did something happen with your girl?"

I grit my teeth, the corners of my eyes stinging. After clearing my throat, I take a sip of ice water. "Turns out she's not my girl after all."

Esther makes a small, sympathetic sound, reaching out to take my hand across the table.

I'm so tired from staying up drinking all night, I've pretty much lost every ounce of pride and self-control I had left. I've never felt more helpless in my life, and I know that Esther is the kind of woman who will truly listen.

"I quit my job yesterday. You'll be the last client I'll ever see. This job is the only thing I've ever been good at, and I quit so I could be with her. Stupid, right? Like quitting would make up for all the things that I've done."

Esther squeezes my fingers. "What did she say when you told her?"

"I didn't get the chance. Her friend told her about me before I could. She never knew what I did for a living—until her friend told her. Now she won't talk to me. And I get that. I was a complete idiot to think that someone like her would want to be with someone like me. And the worst part is that I was so ready to change. Spending time with Elle showed me the kind of person I want to be, the kind of life I want to have. But it turns out that none of that was real. At the end of the day, I'm just a male whore who fell for one of his clients."

"Oh, Nic, don't say those things about yourself. You have so much to offer. Any woman who can't see past your job is a fool."

"I just wish I could talk to her. I know it's stupid, but I think if I could have just been the one to tell her, she would understand. And I wouldn't feel so goddamn hopeless right now."

"If that's true, then you should go."

I snap my gaze up to Esther, who's looking at me with a mix of kindness and sadness. "What do you mean?"

"If there's one thing I've learned in this life, it's that the people we love matter more than anything else in the world. Put your pride aside. Make her understand how you feel."

I slowly shake my head, pulling my hand from hers. "Esther, I don't know—"

But she simply raises her hand to silence me, the next words out of her mouth lighting a fire in me I didn't even realize had gone out.

"Go fight for your girl. Fight for the future you want. No one's going to hand it to you, honey. Go get it."

A lump of emotion lodges itself in my throat. "What about dinner?"

She waves a hand at the menus resting between us. "Truth be told, I'm sick of this place. I just liked the company."

I chuckle and rise to my feet. "I'll miss you, Esther."

"Same here. Now go make me proud."

The smile she gives me is so warm and familiar and comforting, I feel like maybe, just maybe, there's still a chance.

Chapter Nineteen

Elle

It's been a couple of days since I learned what Nic and Christine did, and I still can't believe it. Everything makes so much sense now; there were so many warning signs that I ignored. Even more than their deceit, I'm upset that they made me look like a fool.

Who was I kidding, walking around town like a lovesick puppy, so excited about what I thought was my new amazing relationship with Nic? But, of course, a guy like him would never go for someone like me unless he was being paid. How could I have been so naive?

After I got home from the farmers' market, I spent the rest of the weekend lying in bed—watching reality TV, eating every type of junk food known to man, and feeling sorry for myself.

Today, I'm forcing myself to rejoin the world. I take an extra-long shower, put on makeup, and dress in a cute outfit. They say if you look good, you feel good, right? Besides, I'm a firm believer in tough love, and in all honesty, my solo pity party was getting pathetic.

My phone buzzes in my pocket as I leave my apartment, and I pull it out. It's Nic again. He's been calling me nonstop, but I haven't answered. I don't know what he has to say for himself, and right now I don't care. Lying to me continuously for weeks isn't something I can forgive easily, and I'm not ready to just sweep this under the rug.

I try not to think about Nic as I drive to class. It's the first day of the bar review sessions he enrolled me in, and after three hours of mentally going back and forth, I decided to still attend, especially since I already took the day off work. I'm determined to see this through, and I won't let Nic take my pride *and* my chance at becoming a lawyer.

I blast '90s pop songs as I drive, and by the time I get to class, I'm already feeling better. It's amazing what a little Britney Spears and some fresh air can do for your mood.

Nervous, I take a seat, feeling like a teenage girl on her first day of high school. I'm finally starting to follow my dreams, and even though I'm excited, it's still a whole lot intimidating. Luckily, the teacher is a sweet older woman who knows what she's doing. Somehow, I'm able to get Nic off my mind for a few hours while we discuss the bar exam and go through some study techniques.

As I push the front door open after class, I stop in my tracks. I do a double-take to make sure I'm seeing right. Nic is standing next to my car.

My heart starts to pound, and I think about turning around and going back inside. He hasn't noticed me yet; I could still get away without talking to him.

Get a grip, Elle, you're a grown woman.

What am I going to do, hide every time I run into him for the rest of my life? I need to face him sometime.

Despite how much I don't want to be around Nic, I can't stop myself from noticing that he looks sinfully sexy. A few days apart almost made me forget about his chiseled jawline and strong cheekbones.

He betrayed you, remember?

I chastise myself, determined not to lose my resolve to be angry with him simply because he can pull off a casual T-shirt and jeans better than just about anyone.

He's leaning against my passenger side door, his hands in his pockets. As I approach, he looks up and our eyes meet. I hate that those dark brown eyes can still make my stomach flip, even after everything we've been through.

"What are you doing here?" I ask, keeping some distance between us. Even though I can't stop my overactive libido from spiraling out of control around him, I'm still in touch with the sane part of my brain that's pissed at him for lying to me.

"Sorry to ambush you like this, but you wouldn't answer my calls." He's watching me carefully, but I don't budge.

"What is there to say?" I ask, throwing out my arms in exasperation. "You lied to me."

"I know," he says quietly. "And you have no idea how much I regret that. Would it be okay if we go somewhere and talk?"

I think about saying no, about just walking away and never speaking to him again. But then I think about all the sweet moments we've had, and all the things he's done for me. I sigh, nodding. The least I can do is hear his side of the story. I owe it to myself to at least try to understand.

Luckily, there's a coffee shop next to the review class, and we head in and find a table. Once we're settled, Nic takes a deep breath.

"Elle, the truth is that the weekend I spent with you was more than just a job. From the moment I first saw you, something was different."

"Why should I believe that?" I ask, not meeting his eyes. "You lied about everything else. Do you know how stupid this makes me feel?"

"Look, I know I don't have a ton of credibility right now, but after that first weekend, I stopped seeing clients." He runs his hands through his hair. "I barely knew you, but after our kiss, I couldn't stand the thought of being with another woman. So I resigned, and I have no idea what I'm going to do for money. It's fucking terrifying, but the thought of going back to that job, to the way I used to live, isn't something I can stomach. Not after meeting you."

I keep staring at my cup of coffee, trying to detect if anything he's saying is bullshit. He seems completely genuine and honest, but I'm still afraid to believe him.

"You showed me that sex is more than just a transaction," he says, his voice becoming more urgent. "I'd never felt anything like that before. I've fallen in love with you, Elle."

I finally look up and meet his gaze, and I can see his eyes are full of emotion. Somehow, I know with absolute certainty that despite whatever lies he told in the past, in this moment he's being completely sincere. Being the real Nic.

"You showed me what love felt like, and it's been missing from my life for so long." Nic reaches out and places his hand on mine.

I'm so overwhelmed and shaken, my eyes fill with tears. I still haven't said anything. My mind is going a million miles a minute, and I'm in total shock.

He loves me?

"Will you forgive me?" he asks, squeezing my hand. His touch sends electricity up my arm, and my heart skips a beat as I stare at him.

"You were going to tell me?" I ask finally, trying to keep my voice from cracking.

"Of course. I was coming to tell you that day, but Christine beat me to it. I was only waiting to make sure I had everything in order first. I broke every rule I had for myself—before you, I'd never kissed a client, and I was . . ." He stops and pushes his hands into his hair.

"What?" I ask, now curious. I'm also completely surprised that he's never kissed a client before. It probably shouldn't, but it makes me feel special somehow.

He shakes his head. "It was stupid."

"Tell me, Nic."

"I didn't kiss on the mouth."

"Never?" I ask.

"Never."

His deep voice hits me straight in the chest. Remembering our first kiss at the wedding makes my heart ache.

"And . . . I was saving oral sex for the girl I was in love with."

His words take a moment to register. "*Seriously*? You never went down on a client before?"

He shakes his head, his sad eyes meeting mine.

Even though I should still be mad, should be

disgusted with his career choices, part of me just feels sad. Sad for him, this sweet, broken man who gave me his heart so easily, who left the only world he knew for a shot at love. When I think about the women who have hired him, think about him playing some fantasy role but always holding part of his true self back, it makes my throat tighten. It's then I know that I can't stay mad at him.

"I never did anything like that with anyone before. It was you, Elle. You made me want to break all my rules. Only you."

I nod, taking in his words. I know Nic's a good person, and he's trying really hard right now to make amends.

"If we're going to do this, if I forgive you, I want it all. I want to be a part of your life; I want to meet your parents. I want this to be for real."

He smiles at me. "You want to meet my parents?"

I stare into his eyes. "Of course I do."

He nods. "You can have anything you want if you'll be mine."

I lean toward him and run a hand through his thick hair. He tilts my chin up and gives me a sweet, gentle kiss. It feels so good to be with him that I know this is the right decision. Lately, I've been all about taking more risks, and while this is a big one, I know it's what I need to do.

"Let's get out of here." Nic stands and grabs my hand, and we walk outside together.

"Do you want to come over?" I ask as we reach the parking lot.

Nic nods, throwing an arm around my shoulder. He pulls me in for another tight hug before we get into our cars, and the whole ride home, I'm grinning to myself.

I'm going to be with Nic, for real. No secrets, no lies, no questions. Just us.

We meet outside my apartment, and I walk up to his car as he parks.

"So that explains the fancy car, then," I say, realizing for the first time why Nic can actually afford his lifestyle.

He laughs. "Yeah, I guess the job did have some perks. Although, I'll probably have to sell it now."

I put my arms around him. "Whatever happens next for you, I know you'll be great," I say, burying my face in his chest. "Besides, I'll be there to help."

When I lift my gaze to stare into his eyes, he shakes his head with a smile. "How'd I get this lucky?"

"Just wait until you see what I have planned for you later," I say with a wink, turning to walk inside.

"I think I have an idea." He smirks, giving my butt a slap.

We laugh, and as I walk into my apartment, I can't help but think how far we've come from the first time he came here. I smile to myself, thinking how embarrassed I was about getting too drunk, and how understanding he was about it.

"Take a seat. I have a bottle of malbec in the kitchen," I say, gesturing for Nic to sit on the couch. I pour us each a glass of wine and hand one to Nic, settling in next to him.

"Your apartment looks even better than before," he says, looking around the room. "Or maybe it's just more pleasant in here because you aren't puking in the bathroom right now."

"Hey," I say in mock offense as he smirks at me. "I think after the other day, we're even when it comes to the drinking."

"Touché." He grins.

"So, that night, after the wedding, did you actually want to sleep with me? Or were you just trying to make sure I had fun?" I ask tentatively. I believe he does love me, but you can't blame me for being curious about some of the details.

"You have no idea how much I wanted to." He rubs the back of his neck with his hand. "I felt so bad that you were sick, but in a way, I was relieved, because I knew it would be wrong to sleep with you."

I nod, everything making more sense now. "I know you probably don't want to talk about it, but I have to ask." I bite my lip. "Why'd you take the escort job in the first place?"

"I want to be completely honest with you, so feel free to ask anything," he says, watching me intently. "The escort thing just kind of happened. My friend owns the company, and he offered me the job. I was a natural, and the money was so good that I stuck around and never really had a reason to leave." He pauses. "Until you."

I swallow as I listen. It makes sense, and honestly, who am I to judge his choices?

"What about everything you told me about your dreams? Do you really want to build houses?"

"That part was all true," he says, nodding. "It's always been my dream."

"Then you should do that," I say, and take a sip of my wine. "Remember our pact? I'm taking the bar after this review course is over, so it's time you hold up your end."

"Well, I can't break the pact now, can I?" He smiles, staring into my eyes again.

I scoot closer to him so our bodies are touching. When our lips meet, electricity shoots through me. My lips part as his tongue enters my mouth, and I grip the back of his head. He moves his hands along my arms, sending a shiver through me and straight between my legs. He grabs my hips, pulling me closer against him, and I let out a quiet moan.

I'm totally consumed by him, and it's like I'm kissing him for the first time again. But it's even better, because this time it's all real.

Chapter Twenty

Nic

I pull Elle closer, relishing the feel of her body pressing into mine, our limbs intertwining. We strip each other down to our underwear, so slowly and carefully, it feels like my heart might explode. Every single one of my nerve endings wants me to just rip her clothes off and ravage every inch of her skin.

But after what we've been through, how much she's willing to overcome to be with me, I know I need to take this one slowly. I need to show her how much she means to me, how much her forgiveness means.

She reaches for the waistband of my briefs, her fingertips dipping below the elastic, but before she can find her target, I take both her hands in one of mine. Guiding her body until her back is against the wall, I raise her hands over her head. I want to worship every part of her.

"Not yet, baby," I murmur, my lips at her throat.

With my free hand, I unhook her bra and let it fall to the floor. Bringing my mouth to her neck, I suckle on her tender skin while massaging her full, round breast, gently teasing her nipple. Elle lets out a little moan, trying to free her hands to touch me, but I hold them in place. I want her to touch me— of course I do. But right now, this isn't about that. This is about her.

Elle whimpers in frustration, trading the use of her hands for the use of her body. She wriggles against me, rolling her hips into the growing bulge by my thigh. My cock twitches at her touch, causing a low groan to escape from deep within me, and I smile against her neck.

Clever girl. Looks like I really have met my match.

Releasing her hands from over her head, I take two handfuls of her ass and lift her into the air. She instinctively wraps her legs around my waist, her arms following suit around my neck. Our lips meet with more urgency this time, our tongues dancing around each other as I walk us to the bed. She runs her fingers through my hair, her nails dragging over my scalp and neck, sending a chill down my spine.

When we reach the bed, I gently place her on her back. Slowly peeling her panties away from her body, I leave a trail of kisses down her hips and legs. Once they're off, I step out of my briefs, releasing my rock-hard cock. Elle smiles hungrily at the sight, propping herself on her elbows so her perfect breasts are on full display.

"God, Nic . . ."

I lower my body over hers, my hands resting on either side of her as our lips meet, the supple skin of her breasts brushing against my chest. I turn to lie on my side and Elle does the same, our legs intertwining, my cock pressing into her stomach.

Our kisses deepen, my hand tangling in her hair as I guide her mouth over mine. Her body begins writhing in rhythm with our kisses, her skin rubbing against my erection, driving me absolutely crazy.

Sliding my hand down over her body, I slip a finger between her legs, gently caressing her. She's so wet, I'm immediately even more turned on. Dipping two fingers inside her, I pump them slowly in and out, moving my mouth to her chest as Elle throws her head back with a low moan.

As I continue working in and out of her center, she brings a warm hand to my cock, spreading the few beads of pre-cum over the head. I let out a low groan as she pulls along the length of my shaft, sending a shock wave through my whole body.

Elle comes within moments, her body tensing around my fingers with her cries. Once her orgasm subsides, I position myself closer and carefully slide inside her, ready to make her come all over again.

"You feel so tight, baby. So good," I say on a groan.

"Nic." She exhales heavily, her eyes locked on mine. "More."

I obey, pumping my hips harder, giving her my full length until Elle's whimpers become moans of pleasure and her body tightens around mine, squeezing and milking me until I follow her over the edge.

We lie there entangled in each other until our breathing normalizes, and I press my lips to her forehead.

"That was fucking incredible."

I rise from the bed and pad naked into the bathroom, where I retrieve a wad of tissues to hand to Elle.

She wipes between her legs, and then rises on her knees to give me a quick kiss before going to the bathroom to clean up. I hear the water running, and she returns a few minutes later and crawls into bed next to me. Curling into my side, she rests her head on my chest.

After a moment, she giggles and looks up at me, amusement dancing in her eyes. "You know, this explains a lot, actually."

I raise an eyebrow and cock my head to the side. "What do you mean?"

"For starters, why you're so good at sex," she says, and we laugh.

I nod, running my fingers through her hair. "I had a lot of it, sure, but it was never like this."

"Like what?"

"Never this good. Never on this level. Trust me, it's so much better with you. Honestly, I didn't know it could be this good."

Elle smiles, lifting her head and pressing her lips to mine. "You're sweet. You're probably also full of shit, but you're sweet."

My expression turns serious and I touch her cheek. "Never doubt this. Us. Fuck, I promise you I've never felt anything remotely this good."

"Nic . . ."

I kiss her again, loving the feel of her smiling against my lips.

We lie there for what feels like hours, laughing and talking and cuddling. I've had a lot of sex, but I've never had this effortless intimacy afterward. I've never been this comfortable with a woman before, and it's perfect. More perfect than I ever imagined it could be.

"Are you sure you're ready for this?"

I stop at the corner outside the upscale diner, taking both of Elle's hands in mine and looking into her eyes.

"For the forty-second time, yes, Nic. I'm sure I'm ready."

"You don't have to just say that, you know. I can call right now and cancel. I'm really good at coming up with last-minute excuses."

Elle smiles, her eyes crinkling a little at the corners like they do when she's being patient with me. "Are you sure *you're* ready for this? You've given me every chance possible to get out of this breakfast since we scheduled it last week."

"Of course I'm ready for this. I just don't want you to feel pressured or uncomfortable or like I'm rushing you—"

Before I can finish, Elle cuts me off with a kiss, giving my hands a reassuring squeeze. When we part, she looks into my eyes, wiping the traces of her lip gloss from my mouth with her thumb.

"I'm exactly where I want to be."

"Well, in that case, let's do this."

We walk hand in hand the few feet to the front door of the diner, and I hold the door open for her. Once we're inside, I scan the room, my gaze landing on the familiar older couple sitting in one of the wooden booths. My parents are already here. Mom has chin-length gray hair and high cheekbones, and Dad has wire-framed glasses and a well-kept gray beard.

My mom sees me first, her eyes lighting up as

a smile spreads across her face. I lead Elle toward them, my heart pounding harder than I thought it would.

Jesus.

When we reach the table, Mom stands and throws her arms around me, squeezing my neck and planting a kiss on my cheek. "Oh, my Nicco, it's so good to see you!" she squeals.

Dad stands to greet us, pulling me in for a quick hug and patting my back.

When we part, I put my arm around Elle, stepping back a bit so they can see her better. "Mom, Dad, this is my girlfriend, Elle."

"Mr. and Mrs. Evans, it's so nice to meet you," Elle says, politely extending a hand.

My father takes it, shaking it warmly. "Please, call me Andrew."

"Sofia," my mother says, pulling Elle in for a big hug.

My father and I exchange glances, and he shrugs. My mother has always been the touchy type. I should have known that today wouldn't be any different.

When my mother finally lets Elle go, the four of us sit, my parents on one side of the booth and Elle and me on the other. Our waitress arrives with waters for the table, and my father orders four coffees and four orders of pancakes.

"I hope you like pancakes, Elle," my father says as the waitress walks away.

"Family tradition," I say, holding her hand underneath the table.

"Pancakes sound perfect," Elle replies, smiling broadly at my parents.

My mother claps her hands together, then leans forward and rests her elbows on the table. "So, Elle, tell us everything. How did you and our Nicco meet?"

"Sofia, give the girl a second to settle in," my father says, but my mother only waves him off.

"Nicco hasn't brought a girl home in years, Andrew. Obviously, this one is special to him."

"Mom . . ."

Elle chuckles and squeezes my hand. "Well, Sofia, I'm flattered to hear you say that. Nic and I met at my brother's wedding, actually. He married my best friend, and Christine is the one who introduced us." She turns and smiles at me, and I smile back at her.

I guess that's all true, right? How the hell did I get so lucky?

"Oh, weddings are so romantic! Nicco, how did you introduce yourself to her? You've always had a way with the ladies. Was she immediately taken with you, or did you have to fight to woo her?"

"Sofia, come on."

"What? I have a lot of questions. I'm sure they have a great story."

Elle and I exchange a look. If only my mother knew the truth.

But before we can come up with a more parent-friendly version of our story, the waitress returns with our coffee and pancakes, and I deftly turn the conversation to other topics. Soon, Elle and my father are deep in conversation discussing law school and legal matters, while my mother grills me on how well I'm protecting our secret family recipes.

Seeing Elle hit it off so well with my parents totally calms my nerves, and I quickly realize how silly it was of me to be nervous. I wouldn't have wanted to introduce her to them if I didn't think they'd get along. Or if I wasn't serious about her.

Even if they hadn't liked her, for whatever stupid reason, I know deep in my heart that that couldn't keep me from her. Being with Elle has totally altered the course of my life, and I couldn't be happier about it.

By the end of brunch, my mother has Elle cornered, fawning over her hair and eyes, and asking her all kinds of questions about whether I'm treating her well.

"If Nicco is ever *anything* but a gentleman to you, just give me a call. I'll be sure to set him straight," my mother says, taking Elle's hands in hers.

"Thank you, Sofia, I really appreciate that. But I think we'll be okay. You have raised an amazing son who is the perfect gentleman."

My mother nods, smiling at me, but turns and gives Elle a serious look when she thinks I can't see.

We stand to leave, my mother looping her arm through Elle's. The two women exit the diner together, laughing and chatting about God knows what. Part of me wants to roll my eyes at my mother, but really, it warms my heart to see them getting along so well.

As we follow them out of the restaurant, my father claps his hand on my shoulder.

"You did good, Nic," he says, watching Elle laugh with my mother.

"Thanks, Dad. I know."

"I haven't seen you this happy in a long time. It makes me happy to watch. You going to marry this one, son?"

I smile as I watch Elle, taking in the way her smile crinkles the corners of her eyes, and how her hair shines in the afternoon sun.

"That's the plan."

Chapter Twenty-One

Elle

I round the corner, following my GPS as I wind through an upscale neighborhood full of large homes. Eventually, I spot the right address and park my car in front of the two-story colonial. The door is partially open, so I let myself in.

My jaw drops as I walk inside and take in the interior. I wander around the house, amazed by the detail in the beautiful crown molding and wood paneling, before finding Nic in the kitchen.

He's bent over the counter, shirtless, putting the finishing touches on the tiles surrounding the sink. I take in the flexed muscles in his back, my stomach doing a little flip that sends shivers straight to my lady parts.

I wait a moment before knocking gently on the

door frame of the kitchen. Nic turns around and smiles when he sees me.

"Perfect timing," he says, setting down his tools. "I just finished the last details on these counters. So, what do you think?" He turns to lean on the counter. "Does it look good?"

True to his promise, Nic used the money he saved up at the escort job to put a down payment on a small house in a nice part of town. The place was in pretty bad shape, but he rebuilt the entire kitchen and bathroom by hand.

He's been working tirelessly for weeks to redo every square inch of a home that most people wouldn't have looked at twice. Now it looks like something straight out of *Architectural Digest.* I figured Nic had talent, but I had no idea he could do all this.

"This is amazing, Nic," I say, surveying the kitchen. I know how much this means to him, and I'm so proud that he pulled it off. "The detail is incredible. I've never seen anything like this."

And it's not just the house that looks good. As I look Nic up and down, I'm tempted to run over to him and throw myself at him right there. The muscles in his stomach and arms have become even more defined after all the carpentry he's been do-ing, and he looks so sexy. I can't believe he's mine.

He runs his hands through his hair. "Do you like these details in the molding? I was choosing between that and something else."

I've never seen Nic this nervous before, and it's kind of cute that he cares so much about what I think of the house. He looks back at me as I walk over to him and put my arms around his neck.

"You did good, kid," I say with a wink, and give him a quick kiss. "I'm sure the new owners will love this molding."

"I'm going to get you all sweaty." He laughs as I lean against him, running my hands along his hard biceps.

"Promise?" I ask with a smirk.

I survey the kitchen one more time. He's in-stalled marble countertops, redid the cabinetry, and handpicked the brushed nickel knobs on the cabi-net doors. Not to mention the pale blue tile back-splash, which he imported from Italy. "You really did all this yourself?"

He nods. "I still can't believe I actually start-ed this business. I never would have gone for it if it weren't for you." He puts an arm around my shoulder and kisses the top of my head. "Seriously, thanks for encouraging me."

I smile up at him. "That's what I'm here for. Besides, you encouraged me to take the bar exam first."

My review class is going well, and I'm on track to sign up take the bar soon. It's crazy to think about where Nic and I were six months ago, and how far we've come.

Being with him has been even more amazing than I imagined it could be, and between all the romantic dinners and weekend getaways, the past few months have flown by. It's safe to say I've fallen head over heels for him, and it feels like I'm living a fairy tale. That is, if a fairy tale ever started off with the hero secretly being a male escort.

"So, how does it feel to have your house sell the first day on the market?"

"Pretty damn good," he says, wiping his hands on a rag. "I feel like I'm finally doing things right."

I give his hand a squeeze as I look out the window. He's even put effort into the landscaping, filling the yard with trees and different kinds of plants.

"So, you're an amazing boyfriend, you like to cook, *and* you can garden?" I ask, raising an eyebrow. "How are you real?"

He laughs, pulling me against him and kissing me. I close my eyes as his hands move to my hips. When I pull back, I bite his lip gently and grin.

"That's right. You're also a damn good kisser."

He laughs. "I should have brought you here sooner. I had no idea I'd get so many compliments."

Smiling, I lay my head on his chest before looking out the window again. He's built a gazebo in the middle of the yard with ivy growing up the sides and benches inside.

"I've always wanted a gazebo just like that," I say, pointing toward it.

"Then I'll have to build you one," Nic says, resting his chin on top of my head.

This isn't the first time we've talked about a future together, but standing with Nic in the house he built, I can imagine it more clearly than ever.

"So it's time to say good-bye?" I ask.

He hasn't let me come by the house before today, wanting to wait until it was finished. Neither of us expected it to sell so fast, so it's time to do the final walk-through before the new owners close on the property.

"Is it weird that I feel kind of sad saying good-bye?" he asks as we wander through the dining room.

"No way. This is your baby," I say, taking his hand in mine.

He nods, gesturing down the hallway. "Come on, I want to show you upstairs."

He leads me up a wooden staircase and through the four bedrooms, each with its own unique detailing. It's obvious how much work Nic put into the house, and I'm so proud that he did all of this, if not with his own two hands, then alongside the crew he hired.

"What are you going to do with the profit? Buy another house?" I ask as we wander into the master bedroom.

The windows are open, and there's a gentle breeze blowing. The sun is about to set, casting a golden glow throughout the room. I let go of his hand to feel the smooth metal of the antique door-knobs that Nic and I found at an estate sale.

"I thought about it," he says. "But there's something more important I need to do first."

"More important?" I turn to him, confused, and see that he's down on one knee holding a small black velvet box.

"Nic!" I gasp, not believing my eyes. This can't be what I think it is.

"Elle," he says, opening the box to reveal a beautifully simple diamond ring. "You've changed my life more than I ever expected. You're the most beautiful, talented, smartest, funniest woman I've ever met. I've been happier since I met you than I have in my entire life, and I never want that to change. I want your face to be the last thing I see before I fall asleep, and the first thing I see every morning. Will you marry me?"

Instantly, tears spring to my eyes. I'm in total shock, but I feel myself breaking into a grin. "Nic . . ." I gasp again, grabbing his hands in mine. "Are you serious?"

I'm in full crying mode, and I don't even try to wipe the tears from my eyes.

"I can't believe it." I sob, pulling Nic up and into a hug.

"Elle," he says, pulling back. "You never said yes."

We both laugh as I nod my head.

"Of course I want to marry you."

Nic grins and slides the ring onto my finger. He pulls me against him and kisses me. I close my eyes and wrap my arms around him, feeling his hard chest press against me. I pull back to wipe my tears away, sure my makeup is completely ruined.

"I can't stop crying," I say, laughing.

"I came prepared."

Nic smirks as he pulls a tissue out of his pocket and hands it to me, just like he did at the wedding. Remembering that moment when we barely knew each other only makes me cry harder.

"It's so perfect," I say after I pull myself together, holding up my hand to admire the ring. It's a princess cut, and the white gold band fits perfectly on my finger. "How did you know to get this ring?" It's the exact ring I've been picturing for years, and only a few people knew about it. Who could have told him?

"Well, I had a little help," he says, pulling me close again and looking into my eyes. "I called

Christine."

My jaw drops. "You and Christine went ring shopping together?" I'm floored.

After I forgave Nic, I called Christine and we made up. I knew she only hired Nic to help me, and she had my best interests at heart.

But even after she and I were back to normal, she was still wary of Nic. I've been trying to get them in the same room for weeks so she can see how amazing he really is, but she kept making excuses not to show up. I'd been starting to wonder if she'd ever be able to move past him being an escort.

"She came around after we talked it through," he says, wiping a tear from my cheek with his thumb.

"What did you tell her?" I've been friends with Christine a long time, and I know how stubborn she can be. I can only imagine what it must have taken to change her mind about Nic.

"The truth," he says. "That from the moment I met you, I knew nothing in my life would ever be the same. And I can't picture spending even one day apart from you. Once she realized this was for real, she was happy to help."

My eyes fill with tears again. I'm so touched that Christine and Nic are able to be close, that I'm feeling emotional all over again. I could never marry someone my family wasn't okay with, and Nic knows how much it means to me that everyone I love sees him the way that I do.

I throw my arms around Nic and jump into his arms, wrapping my legs around his waist and kissing him. "We're getting married," I say, pulling back for a moment. I can't believe it's all really happening.

"All right, waterworks, let's get out of here," he says, setting me on the floor.

I take his hand as we walk out the door. It's one of the first warmer days of spring, and I inhale deeply, taking in the scents of the budding flowers.

I smile up at Nic. We've been through a lot of ups and downs over the course of our relationship, but I've got a feeling we're headed for a happy ending.

Epilogue

Elle

One year later

I roll over onto my stomach, the sun warming my back. When I glance up, I see Nic approaching with a round of drinks, and I smile. My heart skips a beat at the sight of him shirtless, his strong biceps flexing as he sets the frozen drinks down. I almost want to pinch myself, because it all feels like a dream.

"I can't believe we had to come all the way to Bali just to get some alone time," Nic says, sitting on the sand next to me.

"Can we stay here forever?" I ask, then take a sip of my strawberry margarita.

Between Nic getting his business started, me

studying for the bar exam, and planning the wedding, it feels like we've barely seen each other lately. Now, with the wedding and the bar exam behind me, I'm officially an attorney now and have joined a great firm, and we're finally relaxing on our honeymoon. It's been better than I could have ever imagined. Not only did I marry the sexiest, kindest, most thoughtful man in the entire world, but the trip has been perfect so far.

We had the wedding at a beautiful outdoor venue in the country, with both of our families there. True to form, I couldn't hold back my tears throughout the ceremony, but I was so happy, I didn't care. It was absolute perfection, and I almost couldn't believe it was real. But if there's one thing I've learned from being with Nic, it's that not *everything* is too good to be true.

Nic glances at his watch as I take another sip of my margarita. It's delicious.

"I've got a surprise for you in an hour," he says, grinning at me. "So drink up."

"What is it?" I prop myself onto my elbows. I was ready for a long day of lying on the beach doing nothing, but I'm intrigued by the idea of a surprise.

He raises an eyebrow. "It wouldn't be a surprise if I told you. But, trust me, you're going to like it."

Nic lies down on the sand and puts an arm around me. I scoot closer to him and press my lips to his cheek.

Even after the wedding and everything we've been through, I still get butterflies every time I'm close to him. Something about him has always felt like home to me. Warm and familiar and safe. Even when I hardly knew him, the only thing I wanted was more of him. And yes, it's true that when I finally got the full story about his background, it freaked me out a little, but he really is so lovable that I couldn't stay mad at him forever. Plus, it feels a little silly to complain when your husband is one of the most talented lovers in the tri-state area.

After we finish our drinks, we walk to our overwater bungalow to change and head toward Nic's surprise. I watch the beautiful scenery from the window of the car we rented for the week, and he slides his hand into mine.

"So, is Bali everything you imagined?" he asks. We'd gone back and forth about honeymoon destinations, but after seeing some of the pictures online, we knew Bali was the right choice.

"I guess it's okay, if you like perfect weather and beautiful beaches." I grin. "But, seriously, this is like a fairy tale."

He chuckles and places one hand on my bare knee.

"How does it feel being on your first international trip?" I squeeze his hand.

"It's pretty damn amazing. Or maybe it's just being here with you."

"I am pretty amazing, aren't I?" I say, smirking at him.

Nic snorts as he slows the car, finally parking in front of a small hut on the side of the road. I can't tell exactly where we are, but there aren't any signs of life, just a lot of trees and a huge field. I climb out of the car, trying to figure out what we could possibly be doing here. The silence gives me the creeps, and I give Nic a doubtful look.

"Wait here while I check on something," he says, keeping his poker face in place.

I can tell he's loving keeping me on my toes with this surprise, which makes me want to figure it out even more.

"Is the surprise that you're going to have me

killed?" I shout after him, raising an eyebrow.

Nic laughs before stepping inside the hut.

I look up at the sky, which is clear and blue. Whatever we're doing, we couldn't have gotten better weather for it. Between the past few days of snorkeling, hiking through gorgeous scenery, and seeing all kinds of exotic animals, I don't think there's any surprise that could top what we've already been doing.

"They should be here any minute," Nic says, stepping back out of the hut.

"Who?" I ask. I know I should just wait to find out, but I can't help it.

Before Nic can answer, I hear something loud approaching above us. I look into the sky as a helicopter appears and touches down in the field.

I turn to him, gaping.

"This is our ride." He grins.

"Seriously?" I laugh, raising an eyebrow. "We could have just taken the car."

"Not where we're going," he says, taking my hand and pulling me forward.

I've never been in a helicopter, or even on a

small plane, and I can't believe Nic booked this for us.

We climb into the helicopter and get settled in our seats. My stomach is filled with nerves as Nic straps me into the five-point harness. I scream as we take off, but I'm more excited than I am nervous.

Once we're in the air, the scenery is so beautiful that I forget all about my fears. After a few short minutes, we're high enough that we can see the entire landscape laid out before us like an exquisite map.

"This is amazing," I say to Nic through the headsets the pilot gave us.

"Look." Nic points down at the water. There's a group of dolphins leaping through the water below us.

I grab his hand as we watch the dolphins, and I can't help but smile. It's one of the most majestic things I've ever seen, and I'm so glad I'm experiencing this with Nic.

After we've been in the air for about fifteen minutes, the pilot points out a small island, telling us that it's supposed to have the most beautiful beaches in the world. Then the helicopter starts to descend toward the island. I turn to Nic, wondering if this is supposed to happen, but he just winks at me.

I look around in awe as we touch down on the beach. Only once we're on land again does my stomach finally settle. Nic unbuckles his own seat belt and then helps me with mine. When the door swings open, he steps out and takes my hand to help me climb out onto the warm sand.

"Welcome to your private island for the day," the pilot says, and my jaw drops.

It's the most beautiful place I've ever been. It's drenched in sunlight, and the palm trees sway in the slight breeze. The sand is soft under our feet, and the water is shockingly blue.

I turn to Nic, still not sure how he put all this together without me knowing.

"When did you plan this?" I ask after the pilot leaves, promising to pick us up at the end of the day.

"It's just something I threw together." He shrugs and I laugh, putting my arms around him.

"This is by far the sweetest thing anyone's ever done for me." Happy tears build in my eyes, but I blink them away and hug him again.

"It's not over yet," he says, grabbing my hand and pulling me along the beach.

"There's more?"

My mouth drops open. I still can't quite believe Nic rented us a private island. I take in the rocky cliffs surrounding the beach situated next to clusters of palm trees. There's a gentle breeze, and the only sound is the ocean waves lapping at the sand.

I squint down the beach, trying to make out something in the distance. "Is that a bed?" I ask, incredulous.

"Let's find out."

Nic grabs my hand and we walk over to the canopy bed, which is draped in white curtains. A picnic basket of food and a bottle of champagne chilled on ice wait next to it.

"This is insane. I feel like I'm on *The Bachelor*." I turn to Nic and break into a grin, and he laughs.

"I'm not sure if I should take that as a compliment or not."

I nod. "Oh, it's definitely a good thing."

We pop open the champagne and lie back on the bed, watching the ocean. I snuggle into Nic's arms, closing my eyes. It feels so nice to lie here peacefully with him, I never want to leave.

After we finish our glasses of champagne, I climb off the bed, ready to experience everything our private island has to offer.

"Let's go in the water," I say, tugging his arm.

I toss my sundress on the bed, and Nic removes his T-shirt. He follows me as I jog into the ocean, letting the waves crash over my legs. The water is surprisingly warm.

We play in the shallows for a few minutes and then move to deeper water, where I climb into Nic's arms. He lifts me easily, and I lock my legs around his waist. He looks so happy, his posture relaxed, his eyes alight with mischief and his mouth forming a grin.

"I love you," I whisper, pressing my lips to his.

While we kiss, he carries me back to shore, setting me on the sand before lying next to me. I climb on top of him, kissing him and running my hands through his wet hair. My tongue slides into his mouth, and he runs his hand along my hips, pulling me against him. My heart beats hard as he slides his hands up my back, and our kissing becomes more urgent.

I pull back for a second to take him in, smoothing his hair back. He looks so sexy, so tanned and with his hair messy from the ocean, that I'm tempted to pull off my bikini and fulfill my sex-on-the-beach fantasy right here.

"Exactly how private is this island?" I ask, sliding a hand underneath the waistband of his trunks.

Before he can answer, a large wave crashes on the shore, completely soaking us.

I scream and jump up to run farther up the beach. Nic follows, and we grab the towels that have been left for us, and wipe away the water and sand. Then we collapse on the bed together, still laughing. I wrap my arms around him, our legs intertwining.

If someone had told me a year ago that I'd be lying in a bed with Nic on our own private island, I'd have thought they were crazy. But if I've learned anything, it's that some of the best things in life are the ones you never expected.

"It's pretty private," he says, answering my question from before, and places his hand against my waist. "But we've got all day."

I smile at him.

"Do you want something to eat?" he asks.

I nod and sit up in the center of the massive bed while Nic fixes us two plates with fresh tropical fruit, cheese, crackers, nuts, and little cookies that are swirled with caramel.

I take a bite of cheese while Nic pops a whole cookie into his mouth. Everything is delicious, and we eat quietly for a few minutes.

"So, what's going to happen to the guys?" I ask.

"Hmm?" He toys with the ties holding my bikini bottoms in place, and a warm tingle spreads pleasantly south.

"Case and the agency, I mean. Ever since you left. I don't know; I guess I'm just curious." I pop a grape into my mouth and chew, waiting for him to reply.

"You mean, who's satisfying the women of Chicago since your sexy-as-fuck husband got out of the game?"

I toss a pillow at him.

Nic laughs and catches the pillow, stuffing it behind his head. "Well, Case and Ryder got busier when I left, picking up the slack, and the last time I talked to him, Case was trying to hire a new guy. He's actually got a book deal from a major publisher to write a self-help book on having great sex, so he's been putting more of his time into that lately."

"A book deal? That's interesting." I take one more bite, savoring the sweetness of the cookie with the crisp, chilled champagne.

Nic nods. "Yeah. Couldn't help but notice something seemed off with him at the wedding, though."

"What do you mean?"

He shrugs. "Just a feeling I got. I had that same feeling the last time I talked to him too. Something's been going on with him for a while now. You don't know someone as well as I know Case and not notice when something's up with the guy."

I nod. I wonder if it bothered Case to see Nic so happy, to watch him fall in love and get married. I can't help but think deep down that everyone wants to find love, to find that special someone they'd give it all up for, and male escorts probably want that too. Sure, they act tough and are sexy as sin, but sometimes I think they need love more than anyone.

"Sorry," Nic says. "I didn't mean to dampen the mood."

I lean over and press a kiss to his lips. He tastes like champagne, and I smile. "You didn't. I love that you always tell me what's on your mind."

He nods. "Course I do, baby."

I pat his hand. "When we get back, let's have Case over for dinner."

"Sounds like a plan."

Once the food has been put away, we lie back against the pillows again. It's so peaceful here. The sky is a brighter blue than I've ever seen it, and the sun shines brightly overhead, but we're shaded by the white cotton draped over the poster bed. A warm, happy feeling fills me as I nestle in closer to my husband.

"I guess we got our happy ending, didn't we?" I ask, tilting my chin up toward him.

I look into his chocolate-brown eyes, unable to imagine being with anyone but him. I never knew I could love someone this much, and the whole wedding and honeymoon have been a dream come true.

"You know what the best part is?" he asks, pulling me in closer. "This is only the beginning."

I lay my head on his chest, listening to his heart beat. For once, I'm not worried about the future. Actually, for the first time in a long time, I'm not worried about anything at all. I'm just happy to be here with Nic in this moment.

Our story may not be the most conventional, but I wouldn't change a thing about the journey.

Thank you for reading **Boyfriend for Hire**! Up next is Case's story, **The Hookup Handbook**. He begins falling for the one person he can't have—the very off-limits younger sister of his best friend, Ryder. I'm in love with the book, and I hope you'll check it out!

What to Read Next

The Hookup handbook

My love wand is on a strike.

As bad as that blows, pun unintended, it's ten times worse for me. I'm a male escort, but not just any escort, I'm *the* escort. The one with a mile-long waiting list and a pristine reputation that's very well-deserved.

Only now, I'm on hiatus. Because after years of pleasing women all over the city, my man missile decides to get finicky. And the only woman he wants? Someone I can never have—my best friend's younger sister, the nerdy and awkwardly adorable Sienna.

She's working at the agency this summer, keeping me organized, handling paperwork, and most importantly, keeping me on track to finish writing my book about sex and intimacy, which is due to my publisher in thirty days.

She thinks I hate her, that I don't want her here.

The truth is much more twisted. I get hard every time she walks into my office. Her wide blue eyes and pouty mouth drive me wild with desire, and if she stays, I'm not sure how much longer I can stay away from her.

Little Miss Overachiever says she's here to help? Fine. I'm going to put her nerdy, curvy tush to work.

Sneak Preview

The Hookup handbook

Chapter One

Case

"Charlie, you're the best agent in the biz—and you know I love you—but you've got to stop worrying. I have everything under control."

Wedging my phone between my ear and my shoulder, I stand up to stretch my back and rearrange some client folders behind my desk. It's been six months since I signed a book deal with Smith and Collins publishers, and honestly? Things aren't going great. But there's no way in hell I'm letting my agent know that.

"That's all well and good, Case, but your final deadline is in thirty days. Sure you'll have a finished manuscript by then?"

Fuck. Thirty days? When did that happen?

"Listen, I've been an escort for eight years now. You don't get a mile-long waiting list by having no clue what you're doing in the sack. Every man who reads this book will be a fucking sexpert in no time."

"That's what they're paying you for, champ. As long as you deliver."

My stomach churns. If I don't figure something out soon, I'll be completely fucked. I already used the advance they gave me for a down payment on a home for my mother. And more than anything else on the table right now, I can't let that deal fall through.

"I'll buckle down and get it done, okay? I promise. Look, I have a lot of paperwork to process, but I'll talk to you later." I hang up, dropping back into my chair and dragging a hand over the scruff on my face.

You want to know the truth? Thirty days until the deadline, and I got nothing. Nada.

When I signed up to write a book on sex, I thought it would be a piece of cake. And in some ways, it is. I know exactly what I want to say. It's just the whole putting-words-on-a-page thing that's holding me back. Which I realize is kind of the entire fucking point.

My computer dings with a new email, reminding me that I still have a business to run. The email is from another woman hoping to schedule a date, plus a little extra after dessert. She requests me by name—a friend of hers gave her a referral—which only makes the knot forming in my stomach tighten.

I know my line of work is a little out of the ordinary. I'm aware that most guys my age are busting their asses for the man, and that I've got it pretty fucking good. It's not exactly a hardship to fuck beautiful women for a living. Unless the one thing you've always been able to rely on suddenly goes out of commission.

That's right. The last three times I took a woman to bed, I haven't been able to get it up.

Let's get one thing straight: there's nothing wrong with my dick. I still wake up every morning with the little man saluting like a proud soldier.

But when it comes time to actually perform on the job? He's been as limp and lifeless as a dead fish. Not even a twitch in my pants. Which means that unfortunately I've had to come up with an excuse at the last minute to rush out on my most recent dates—and give the ladies a refund, of course—so yeah, my little problem is starting to cost me. And if I'm not careful, it might cost me in more ways than one.

If word gets out that Case fucking Smith can't get a hard-on, I'm finished. Thank God those women don't know each other and won't be able to swap stories. I can't let anything stand in the way of me making it big—something I've been telling myself is just around the corner for months now.

I grew up with nothing, and now I own a home and run a successful business that allows me to employ a half dozen of my friends. Plus, I'm in the process of buying my mom a home close by, something I've wanted to do from the moment I understood what bills were and how difficult it was for us to pay them. My dad split when I was two years old, leaving my mom to work her ass off to keep food on the table and a roof over our heads.

It's always been just the two of us, and it's about time I returned the favor. Business has been booming these past few years, and I'm so close to finally taking care of her, I can practically smell that fresh coat of paint. Only now, out of nowhere, my dick decides not to cooperate. Which is super inconvenient.

But just because I've taken a temporary hiatus from seeing clients doesn't mean I'm not working. When a major publisher offered me a deal to write a book on sex and intimacy, I jumped at the chance. I've slept with more women than I care to remember, and if there's one topic I know better than any other, it's sex. This book should be a piece of cake—if I can just find a way to sit my ass in front of a computer and type.

A quick knock on the door snaps me out of my thoughts, and in strolls Ryder, my best friend and one of my employees. Frankly, I'm surprised he even knocked. Most of the time, he strolls in like he owns the damn place.

"Hey, do you have a sec?"

"Ryder Johnson in my office before ten? This must be important."

He makes a face and plops down in the chair opposite my desk, swinging one arm over the back. His tousled dark blond hair is pushed back off his forehead, and the scruff that normally lines his jaw is gone, which can only mean one of two things. Either he has a date later—and I'm on top of my employees' schedules enough to know that's not the case—or he wants something. Bad.

"Nah, dude, I just wanted to come say hey, see what you're up to."

I fold my hands and rest my elbows on the desk, raising a single eyebrow.

He smirks. "Fine, you're right. I have a favor to ask."

"Lay it on me."

"I was wondering if you could give my sister a job for the summer. Light office work or something like that. She just graduated from college and needs a way to make some money while she figures out her next move."

I sigh, running one hand through my hair as the computer dings with new emails. "Look, Ryder, I don't know. If I go around employing everyone's little sister that needs a job . . ."

"I get that, but look, she's not just my little sister. She's, like, wicked smart. Super organized, crazy driven, totally type A. We don't really have anyone managing things, and I think she could help out around here."

He has a point. As if the stacks and stacks of paperwork on my desk didn't already make that clear.

"Sure, why not. She can start Monday."

"Really? No interview or anything? You're giving her the job just like that?"

"What, now you're telling me she's not really up for the task? If she's as smart and organized as you say, this job should be mind-numbing for her."

"Thanks, man, I really appreciate it."

"Don't mention it. Now, go find a way to make that fresh shave of yours actually useful."

Ryder smiles, nodding at the schedule open on my computer. "Got a new client for me, boss?"

"Actually, I think I do. I'll send you the deets later today."

He nods and saunters out of my office, probably to play video games and eat my food. Not that I really care. When it comes down to it, he's good at his job. Having a six-pack and God-given good looks makes it easy.

I lean back in my chair and take a long look around the office.

Ryder's right. We could use some help on the administrative front. I've always managed that side of things myself, but with how busy we've been lately, it's been harder and harder to stay on top of it all. Add a book deadline to the load, and I could very well let one too many things fall through the cracks.

Besides, who knows what this girl's major was in college? Maybe she can help me out with this book. God knows I could use the help.

Chapter Two

Sienna

"Can you slow down, Ryd? I really don't want to be late for my first day because you got us pulled over." I have to practically yell for him to hear me over the unrecognizable electronic music he's blaring.

Ryder snorts, rolling his eyes at me. "I do this drive pretty much every day, and I've never once gotten a ticket," he says bluntly, not easing off the gas for a second. "We're fine. Chill out."

When I was a little girl, I was always changing my mind about what I would be when I grew up. I spent countless hours playing princess, teacher, or astronaut. I'd dress up as a ballerina or pretend to be a veterinarian with my stuffed animals, letting my imagination run wild with possibilities of my future career. Mom always told me I could be anything I wanted to be.

Somehow, I don't think working at a male escort agency is what she had in mind, and I can't say it's really at the top of my list, either.

I don't mean to sound ungrateful. Freshly graduated with a business degree and practically zero ideas as to what I want to do with it, any job is better than no job at all. I'm lucky that my brother was willing to vouch for me and get me this part-time gig at his, um, place of employment. *If you can call it that*. I'm doubly lucky that he let me move into his spare bedroom. Not that I can't afford my own place, but it's nice to have a roommate I can carpool with. No way could I walk into my first day at this kind of job without a little moral support.

Ryder zooms through our morning commute, taking every turn a little too fast and paying more attention to his playlist selection than the road. He's been working as an escort with this agency for a few years now, and based on his lazy one-handed grip on the wheel, I'd say the drive is second nature to him. As he swings into a particularly sharp turn, I roll up my window to keep the humid summer air from ruining my carefully styled waves.

But Ryder's right—I do need to chill out. I've got that feeling in my stomach like I'm waiting in line to go on a roller coaster. But who could blame me? It's my first day of work at a job where I'm the only employee who isn't having sex for a living. Ryder's line of work never bothered me much, but I was always able to keep the details at arm's length. Now I'll be right in the middle of the action, so to speak, and I can't help but feel a little grimy about the whole thing.

"You seem tense," Ryder says, turning down the volume on the radio. "Are you thinking about Evan or something?"

Now it's my turn to roll my eyes. I never should have told Ryder about my breakup with my college boyfriend. Now he brings it up all the time, like he thinks he's supposed to ask about it or something. I spared him the real details, like the real reason Evan ended things with me. I also left out the part about my personal goal to chase Evan's memory away with a summer fling.

"No, I'm not thinking about Evan. I'm way over him. That was months ago. I'm just nervous about my first day. This isn't exactly a typical job, you know."

"You'll be great," Ryder says. "And I promise it's not nearly as awkward as you think it's going to be. Case is fuckin' awesome."

Okay, then. Apparently, my new boss is fucking awesome. *Yay, me.*

I pick at a loose thread on my charcoal-gray pencil skirt, hoping Ryder is right. I just have to think of this like any other temporary office job. Just something to buy me time and give me a little experience while I sort out whether to apply for grad school. It'll look good on a résumé, as long as I leave out the company's details.

"Just administrative work, right?" I ask, verifying for what has to be at least the hundredth time.

"Of course. Filing some paperwork, helping the boss stay organized. No funny business. You're just here to work." Ryder takes his hand off the wheel to lay it on his heart, then puts three fingers up in the air. "Scout's honor."

The car veers a bit, and I grip the dashboard for dear life.

"Any way you can put your 'scout's honor' on getting us to the office without crashing the car?"

Ryder returns his grip to the wheel, and my blood pressure returns to normal. "We're not gonna crash," he says as he makes one last sharp turn down what looks more like an extra-long residential driveway than an office entrance. "Besides, we're already here."

As we cruise down the driveway, an enormous white stucco-and-glass home emerges from behind the sycamore trees. Ryder swings the car into a miniature parking lot off to the side of the house, parking next to a small collection of luxury cars.

"Quite the office," I say in a hushed voice, taking in the gorgeous landscaping.

"The office is the entire first floor. Otherwise, it's the boss's house." Ryder unbuckles his seat belt and hops out.

"More like the boss's mansion," I mutter, following Ryder's lead out of the car and up the limestone walkway. I'm wobbling a bit in my black heels but keep my chin high, repeating my brother's promise over and over in my head. *No funny business. You're just here to work.*

Ryder punches in a pass code at the door, and with a whir and a click, we're in. "It's 1022," he says over his shoulder. "Case's mom's birthday. But I'll pretty much always be here with you, so you probably don't have to memorize the code."

I smile, knowing that I'll commit it to memory anyway. I'm not one to let the details slide.

My heels clack along the white marble floor as I follow closely behind Ryder, avoiding eye contact as he greets a tall, toned man who walks by, and then another and another.

"Do I need to know them?" I whisper.

Ryder laughs. "Not if you don't want to. They're just the other escorts. The only one you really need to know is Case."

Past the kitchen and then a conference room, Ryder leads us to a big wooden door and knocks twice. A low, gravelly voice comes from the other side, telling us to come in. And we do.

"Hey, Case, this is Sienna. Sienna, this is the big man, Case."

I step out of Ryder's shadow and lock eyes with Case's ultra-serious stare. Big is the correct adjective to describe this man. He's sitting so I can't properly gauge his height, but he's got to be six and half feet tall. Dressed in jeans and a white T-shirt that his biceps are trying to escape from, he makes me feel overdressed. His coffee-colored hair is short and neat, just like the scruff hugging the angle of his jaw.

He's handsome, there's no denying it. I guess his profession suits him. But it's the stare that catches me the most off guard. So serious and unwavering. His hands are folded neatly on his wooden writing desk next to an overwhelming stack of paperwork, which I can only assume will become my responsibility.

"Sienna. Welcome."

Welcome? That's it? Not a "nice to meet you" or anything? I pause, expecting him to stand up, shake my hand or something, but he doesn't move an inch. Neither does his stare, which is pointed at me with laser-like intensity.

"Happy to be here," I say quickly to fill the silence, although I'm not sure that I mean it. In this moment, I'd rather be anywhere but here. My insides feel like they've been twisted with a fork.

"There's a lot for you to do," he says, nodding towards the paperwork without letting his stare falter. As his attention turns from me to my brother, he relaxes a bit, his tone going from aggressive to friendly. "Ryder, have you checked your email? There's a client for you today. One of your regulars from across town, I think."

Ryder pulls out his cell and nods, scrolling through his in-box. "Shit, this is in like an hour. I gotta head out." He glances up at me. "You all good here? I gotta bounce."

"She's fine," Case says sharply. "I'll get her set up. You go ahead."

I want to beg Ryder not to leave me just yet, but he's the reason I'm getting a paycheck, so I can't stand in the way of him getting his. "Just don't forget you're my ride home, okay?"

Ryder nods. "Of course. I'll for sure be back before the end of the day. Later, guys."

"Later," Case says, the last bit of his casualness fading with Ryder's exit. His eyes move back into that intense stare as he turns back to me. "I guess we should get you started," he says flatly, as if giving me work is a chore for him.

How can he be so friendly with my brother and so icy with me?

Case gets up from his desk, revealing a well-fitted pair of jeans that encase one of the nicest backsides I've ever seen on a man. He's just as tall as I expected. Well over six feet, for sure, which ups the intimidation factor.

Scooping up the pile of paperwork, Case struts over to a smaller desk on the other side of the room. "You'll work here," he says matter-of-factly and plops the paperwork on the desk, sending a few pages flying off the stack. "And this will be your first project. Digitizing these old client files. There's a laptop in the drawer you can use to type them into a spreadsheet. Your brother says you're smart, so I'm guessing you can figure it out."

In a matter of moments, he returns to his desk and is right back to work. And back to ignoring me.

Nice to meet you too. I take my place at my new desk. As the laptop boots up, I pick up the file folders and flip through the paperwork he's given me. Guess it's time to get to work. Only, I can't focus.

For some strange reason, I'm hyperaware of this man sitting just feet from me. Shouldn't we talk? Discuss our goals? What we each want to get out of my employment here?

The longer I sit here inputting customer files, the more agitated I become. I mean, seriously, the guy couldn't even take two seconds out of his day to properly train me? I don't even know where the freaking bathroom is. I have no idea what I'm supposed to do for lunch.

After I've input the twelfth customer file, I pause and take a deep breath. I can feel Case's presence looming like a shadow across the room.

"So . . ." I pause, my attempt at small talk already crashing and burning. "You sleep with women for a living."

Shit. Real smooth, Sienna.

Case doesn't even look up from his computer screen, clearly not thrown by my question. "Sometimes," he says, his deep voice rumbling.

Sometimes? What the hell is that supposed to mean? Isn't that his job?

"How long have you been doing this?"

He thinks about it for a second, still not looking at me. "Eight years, give or take."

"Do you have a girlfriend?"

"No girlfriend."

"Have you ever been in a serious relationship?"

Something like wounded pride or anger flashes through his dark gaze as it briefly meets mine; I'm not sure which. "Not answering that."

Case doesn't want to talk, that much is obvious, but I'm on a roll now.

"I get why Ryder does it, but you— I mean, you run a successful business. Obviously, there's a brain knocking around in that skull somewhere." I try to smile, but my attempt at a joke doesn't just crash and burn, it erupts into a fiery volcano threatening to take me with it.

He looks more annoyed that I made it sound like they're drug dealers or criminals, or possibly because I implied he must be stupid. Which I don't really believe; it just came out wrong.

"Don't kid yourself," he says sharply. "Fucking is what I'm good at. But tell me, why *does* Ryder do it?"

"Basically? To piss our parents off. He's always been a manwhore, and this way he can get paid for what he was doing already without having to blow through his trust fund."

Case's easy expression falters. Maybe he didn't know Ryder has a trust fund. I assume he knows we come from money, and I assume he now knows that I have a trust fund too. I just hope he doesn't judge me for it. As far as I'm concerned, that's my parents' money, not mine. And I intend to work for what I have.

"I like to fuck. It's really that simple, Sienna."

The sound of my name leaving his lips makes my lungs constrict with something hot and uncomfortable.

"Nothing is that simple." And if he actually believes that, he's an idiot. "What's your end game?"

"My what?" His expression is part mild irritation and part amusement at my fifty questions. He turns his big body away from the desk so he's facing me.

"I'm just trying to put the pieces together here." I tap my pen on my knee.

He sits back in the chair and folds his hands behind his head, which makes his biceps look huge. A slight grin tilts his full lips. "Tell me everything that's on your mind. All at once."

"I'm not sleeping with you." Oh my God. Did I just say that? Out loud? Fuck!

"Never asked you to."

I swallow the lump that's now lodged in my throat. "I'm here to work. That's it. I don't want to hear about your conquests. I don't want to know what goes on when you leave here for appointments. The only thing I'm here to do is to help you in this office."

"Perfect. Then we're on the same page."

"Oh, and since I graduated at the top of my class from a top-tier university, I'd appreciate something more challenging than data entry."

He smirks at me. "I'll keep that in mind."

"I guess I'll get to work, then."

Turning back to my laptop, I take a deep breath. I know I've completely overstepped my bounds, and I have no idea why I lost my shit on him.

I open a browser and pull up my email to fire off a quick message to my best friend, Allison.

To: Allison Garner

From: Sienna Johnson

Subject: First Day of Work

I've been in the "office" (more of a mansion— I'll explain later) for all of an hour, and I think my boss already hates me. Best part? My desk is five feet away from him. Remind me why I'm doing this again?

Before I can even open a new spreadsheet to continue with my task, my email dings with a response from Allison.

To: Sienna Johnson

From: Allison Garner

Subject: Eyes on the Prize

To fill time between worrying about grad school and chasing down a summer fling. That's why you're doing this. Don't lose sight of your goals, girl. Give your boss the finger for me. We'll drink about it soon.

A giggle escapes me at the thought. Flipping off my boss my first day on the job? Talk about the fast lane to getting fired.

"What's so funny?" Case gives me a suspicious look from behind his computer monitor.

"Oh, just an email." I close the browser, just in case that intense stare can see through the back of my laptop. "Sorry. I'm halfway through these files now. I know you're trying to work."

"Great," he says curtly, his attention returning to his screen. "Thank you."

I hold tightly to that thank-you, making certain I don't forget the way it sounds in his low, rumbling voice. Something tells me I'm not going to hear it a lot.

Chapter Three

Case

Normally, I'm not the kind of man who has trouble focusing. Half the reason I've been so successful is because when it comes down to it, I buckle down and do what needs to be done.

For the past eight years, I've run this business on my own, managing half a dozen hotheaded men, filing paperwork, being every woman's fantasy in the bedroom, all while putting out client and publicity fires left and right. This business has been my life, my baby, and if there's one thing I have trouble with, it's control. Or rather, giving it up.

And Ryder's goody-two-shoes, whip-smart little sister isn't making that any easier for me. It's only Wednesday, and she's driving me crazy.

"I finished cleaning out your in-box, and I've

organized it so that all incoming emails will go to their respective files. One for clients, one for press, one for employees, and one for everything else."

Sienna barely even takes a breath as she explains it all to me, her blue eyes glued to the computer screen as she clicks from file to file.

"It'll take a few days for the new system to fully adjust, but I'll keep an eye on it. In the long run, it should make your job a lot easier."

When I decided that she should work with me in my home office, it made sense at the time. The room is big enough for both of us to work comfortably, and having her nearby makes it easier to communicate what needs to get done and answer any questions she might have.

But something about having her so close all the time makes my skin crawl. And it's not just because she blows through every assignment I give her in a fraction of the time I think it'll take her. No, being this close to her is unnerving for a whole different set of reasons.

First, I never expected her to be drop-dead gorgeous, with honey-colored hair down to her waist, big blue eyes, and a nice set of perky tits that are definitely more than a handful.

And what is that scent? I've been trying to place it all week. My office usually smells like male deodorant and coffee. Now that's been replaced with a new mouth-watering aroma that I'm having trouble putting my finger on. It's not too flowery or too strong, and there are hints of rose and cedar. She smells chic and sophisticated and utterly sexy.

It's pissing me right the fuck off.

That tongue-lashing she gave me on her first day was more than a little eye-opening. This girl's got balls, that's for sure. She doesn't act one bit like I expected her to, and I have no idea why that's so appealing to me.

Fuck. I scrub my hands through my hair.

I guess it's because I'm used to women fawning all over me, wanting to fuck me from the word *hello*. Sienna is nothing like the women I'm used to. Which is a good thing, I remind myself. If there's one thing I definitely can't do, is picture myself fucking Ryder's little sister.

When my cock twitches in my jeans at the thought, I inhale deeply, trying to calm myself. At the same time, I realize Sienna is looking up from her computer, staring directly at me.

"Thanks for that," I reply, thumbing through

the stack of client files that have somehow tripled behind my desk.

She doesn't respond, and even with my back turned, I can practically see her staring expectantly at me, just like she has every time she finishes a task before I'm ready for her to. So far I've chosen to ignore her, make her say something before giving her something else to do.

I've run out of small, meaningless tasks to give her, and when it comes to throwing real work her way? Well, let's just say I'm not sure I'm ready to do that yet.

After a couple more minutes of silence, she clears her throat, absentmindedly tapping her pen on the pad of paper next to her laptop.

I slowly turn from my paperwork, making a point to meet her gaze. "Yes?"

"Well, I was just wondering, when are you going to let me do something real?"

"Something real?"

"Everything you've had me do so far is grunt work. The kind of thing you have some airhead intern do. I don't know what my brother told you, but I graduated summa cum laude, so I'm sure I can handle something more substantial than data entry, alphabetizing folders, and in-box organizing."

When I finally look up from the stack of papers in my hands, I'm surprised by how stern and direct her gaze is. For someone on the third day of a crappy summer job, she's really not fucking around.

"Plus," she says, sitting up straighter in her seat, "I should know how to run the office when you're not here. For, you know, when you're out meeting with clients." She gives me a double wink. The little brat.

I don't bother pointing out that I'm not currently seeing any clients because that would only prompt her to ask why. I shudder, remembering our game of fifty questions from her first day. She's a nosy little thing without many boundaries, or personal filters, apparently. And I'm certainly not ready to tell anyone, least of all her, that I can't get my joystick to function properly.

"All right, fine. You can take over these new client files. Don't forget to attach the disclaimers and the privacy agreements. The last thing we need is a publicity shitstorm just because the new hire isn't familiar with the rules of the trade."

Sienna nods and flashes me a smile, but I can

tell it's forced. If this job has taught me one thing, it's how to tell when a woman's faking it. And that smile was fake as fuck.

It's week fucking one. What does she want from me? *Christ.*

I drop the new client files on her desk, leaning on the back of her chair and arching a concerned brow. "Look, I'm sure you can handle it. I just don't want to give you more than you can manage to start out. New jobs can be hard enough, and what we do here is so unorthodox, I wouldn't be surprised if you were . . . distracted."

Her eyes grow wide for a moment, a look of horror and disgust quickly taking them over. "If you think I'm going to drool all over you like one of your little groupies, let me assure you, that won't be a problem."

I shrug and cross my arms, stepping back to lean one hip against my desk. I'm about to point out that she couldn't afford a ride on this love stick, but then I remember she said Ryder's a trust-fund kid. Which means she is too. She could probably afford multiple rides on this love stick.

That realization should annoy me, but it doesn't. A familiar ache in my gut throws me off my game for a second, and I notice that Sienna's chest is heaving with frustration. Seeing her so hot and bothered only makes me want to push her further.

"I'm just saying, I wouldn't blame you if working here made it hard to focus."

She sits up straighter and crosses her arms, the upper curves of her breasts just barely peeking out of the neckline of her blouse.

The ache in my gut grows stronger. *What the hell is wrong with me?*

"I don't need to pay for sex," she says quickly, "if that's what you're implying."

"If that's what you think this profession is about, you might as well be some airhead intern."

Sienna scoffs. "Oh, like what you guys do here is so noble."

"You don't think a woman prioritizing her own pleasure and happiness isn't a worthwhile pursuit?"

"Not when it's exploited for monetary gain," she snaps, seemingly pleased with herself.

"Ask any of our clients about their experiences with us, and I assure you, 'exploited' is the last word they would use to describe it. Come to think of it, we have the paperwork to prove it. Let's add filing client-satisfaction forms to your to-do list."

She pauses, a pretty blush creeping over her cheeks and chest.

On a roll now, I take a breath and continue. "I'm sure you're professional enough to handle reading all about how pleased your brother's clients were to take a ride on his . . ."

She holds up both hands. "All right. I, uh, better get to work, then." Grabbing the files I dropped on her desk, she quickly opens the first one and scans the page, the blush lingering on her rosy cheeks.

I return to my desk, feeling satisfied that I won that round. As I sit down, a new email comes in, arriving directly into the EVERYTHING ELSE folder Sienna set up for me. It's Charlie, reminding me for the twenty-seventh time that my deadline for the book is quickly approaching.

"Fuck," I mutter quietly, but clearly not quietly enough.

Sienna nervously raises her head, chewing on her lower lip with her brows knit together. "Did I do something wrong with your email?"

"No, it's not that. My agent, Charlie, has just been all over me lately about this book deal."

Her brows wing upward. "You're writing a book?"

"Supposed to be. The finished manuscript is due in four weeks, and I've got nothing. Well, not *nothing*. But I don't have much."

"Why don't you ask them to extend the deadline? Or just back out? I've seen your finances, and it looks like you're doing fine."

"Can't. Already spent the advance."

"How responsible of you." She rolls her eyes.

Jesus. This girl. She doesn't cut me one ounce of slack.

"On my *mom*."

Sienna must really think I'm an idiot who can't handle his money. At her puzzled expression, I explain.

"I'm trying to move her closer to me, and I already put a down payment on her new place."

"Oh, I'm sorry, I didn't realize . . ."

"Don't be."

I'm about to turn and put my back to her again so I don't have to feel like I've been sucker punched every time I look at her, but I'm struck with an idea. My mouth starts moving before my brain has processed what I'm about to say.

"Actually, maybe you could help me with the manuscript. Ryder said you were good with this kind of stuff."

Sienna side-eyes me. "I stopped writing essays for other people in, like, the eleventh grade."

"No, I don't need that. I know what I want to say. Maybe you could read some of it, point out where it's lacking, help me create a writing schedule so I can stay on track, things like that."

"In that case, Ryder's right. I'm your gal." She smiles, and the ache returns.

Dammit, Case. Get your fucking head on straight.

"So, what about you?" I ask. "I know this job isn't your be-all and end-all. I think Ryder's exact description of you was something like 'the smartest thing since sliced bread.'"

She shifts uncomfortably, a slight smile flickering for a second before it disappears. "Of course

Ryder said something like that. I think I just had an easier time in school than he did. I studied business in college, but by the time I got to the end of it, I wasn't sure about what I wanted to do with my degree. It's not that I didn't enjoy it, it's just . . . never mind."

"Tell me."

She restacks the folders on her desk, not meeting my eyes, but doesn't say anything.

Prompting her, I ask, "So, what do you want to do instead?"

"I'm not really sure yet. I just know I want to be doing something I actually enjoy."

"Like helping keep a male escort on track writing his book on the importance of female pleasure in the bedroom?"

"Something like that, yeah."

We both laugh, and she shakes her head, then tosses her blond locks over her shoulder before returning to her paperwork.

Smart, beautiful, *and* driven? The more I get to know Sienna, the easier it is to forget that she's my best friend's little sister.

It was a relief when she agreed to help me with my book. If her performance so far has made one thing clear, it's that time management is her jam. And it's only her third day.

Suddenly, I don't feel nearly as nervous about meeting my deadline, no matter how worried Charlie might be that I won't follow through.

The only thing making a small knot of worry form in my stomach?

The fact that Ryder's little sister happens to be the only woman who can make my manmeat move.

About the Author

A *New York Times*, *Wall Street Journal*, and *USA TODAY* bestselling author of more than two dozen titles, Kendall Ryan has sold over two million books, and her books have been translated into several languages in countries around the world. Her books have also appeared on the *New York Times* and *USA TODAY* bestseller list more than three dozen times. Kendall has been featured in publications such as *USA TODAY*, *Newsweek*, and *In Touch Magazine*. She lives in Texas with her husband and two sons.

Follow Kendall

BookBub has a feature where you can follow me and get an alert when I release a book or put a title on sale. Sign up here to stay in the loop:

www.bookbub.com/authors/kendall-ryan

Website

www.kendallryanbooks.com

Facebook

www.facebook.com/kendallryanbooks

Twitter

www.twitter.com/kendallryan1

Instagram

www.instagram.com/kendallryan1

Newsletter

www.kendallryanbooks.com/newsletter

Other Books by Kendall Ryan

The Impact of You

Screwed

Monster Prick

The Fix Up

Sexy Stranger

Dirty Little Secret

Dirty Little Promise

Torrid Little Affair

xo, Zach

Baby Daddy

Tempting Little Tease

Bro Code

Love Machine

Flirting with Forever

Dear Jane

Finding Alexei

For a complete list of Kendall's books, visit:

www.kendallryanbooks.com/all-books